RICK & KATJA

THE BIRTH OF A SPY COUPLE

IAN GRIFFIN

The Birth of a Spy Couple

© 2022, Ian Griffin.

Print ISBN: 978-1-66786-050-3
eBook ISBN: 978-1-66786-051-0

Book Cover
Book Baby

Back Photo
Sharon Zambrano

Editor
Joelle Belknap

AUTHOR'S NOTES

This book, in its entirety, is a work of fiction. The book has historical fictional references, but they do not accurately represent the people and figures. It is fiction. Any semblance between real persons and characters, whether they be living or dead, is coincidental. The author in no way or by any stretch of the imagination, represents the companies, places, corporations, political groups, terrorist organizations, individuals, brands, or any other entity imaginable in this book. The author does not speak for or represent anyone, or thing referenced in this book, any likeness of anyone in this book has been used fictitiously. Every opinion the author has expressed in this book is the author's opinion, or to put it bluntly, it is fictional.

DEDICATION

I dedicate this book to several people. First and foremost, to my wife, Wibke, who inspires me daily. I must thank my editor, Joelle Belknap, who was relentless in her editing. She made me a better writer by far. I have to thank T.D. Krupp. We served together for a long time, and he is an established author. My comrade gave me a lot of guidance and inspired me to put my fingers on the keyboard and have fun.

CONTENTS

THE FIRST KILL

"This is the last image you will ever see; it is my blue eyes," Rick lifts his Beretta and aims it at the forehead of his victim. His brown eyes look back at Rick. Maintaining eye contact, Rick pulls the trigger without hesitation. The bullet penetrates the forehead and exits out the back of his skull. His body falls forward to the ground as the smell of gunpowder begins to fill the room. Rick, showing no emotion, looks at the lifeless body lying before him.

On the other side of the bedroom, Katja, naked from the waist down, frantically searches for her pants. She glances at the smoke that slowly billows out from the suppressor at the end of Rick's Beretta and cannot stop shaking as she finally locates her trousers. Katja falls over herself as she works to pull them over her athletic legs. Rick looks at his frantic wife and then looks over at the dead body, surveying his kill.

Katja regains her composure and begins frantically scouring the apartment. She is in such a frenzy that she is stumbling over herself.

"Katja. Katja, what are you doing?" Rick says, trying to get her attention.

"I am trying to find the hard drive. We got to go. We just killed a man," Katja exclaims.

"My love, slow down," he says. "No one knows we are even here. We got time."

"Oh, my love, I went too far, I really went way too far," she says as her voice shakes.

"Katja, no one went too far," Rick says reassuringly. "We all did what we had to do. He was completely off guard. You did that! Let's settle down and find the hard drive. Okay?"

Katja nods her head up and down and catches a glimpse of something out of the corner of her eye.

"Wait, there it is, right there," she said, pointing to a desk on the far side of the living room. "That's his computer and monitor."

Rick looks toward the computer and forms a plan in his mind. "We are leaving the monitor and taking the tower," he decides. "It has the hard drive in it, that's all we need."

A feeling of relief came over Katja as her mood changed for the better.

"Katja, send Franz a note. We need mop up," Rick directs.

"Yes, my love," Katja responds as she begins typing the note. Within seconds, Katja receives a response from Franz.

"They are on their way," she announces.

"Good," Rick replies, then turns to Katja. "My love, I need you to look out the door and make sure no one is in the hallway. If it is clear, we will go down the far staircase, not the one you two came up. You go first and I will follow with the computer tower. Once you are down to the bottom of the stairs, follow me to the car. You got that?"

"Yes, my love," Katja replies, then pauses and thinks for a second. She turns to Rick and says, "wait, Rick." Rick turns to face her. "Let's get his cellphone as well. I mean, he is already dead, and there may be more on there as well," she decides.

"Great idea, Katja," Rick replies.

Katja digs through the man's pockets and finds his cellphone. "Here it is. I got it," she says as she lifts it in the air.

"Good, now let's get out of here," Rick replies.

Katja peaks out the door to the hallway to find it empty. The couple moves quickly down the stairs and to the car. Rick puts the tower in the back seat and helps Katja into the vehicle. He looks around to make sure they were not followed. He gets into the driver's seat, and they head home.

REFLECTION

SEVENTEEN YEARS LATER IN 2021

A slender man around six feet tall, Rick Taylor, takes a familiar trail along the Main River. He has light skin with blond hair, blue eyes and in good physical shape. The river runs from the Bavarian Alps to the Rhine River. Rick happens to be in a spot where the river passes through Kitzingen, a quaint town east of Würzburg, Germany, that is known for producing wine.

Rick steps guide him down a path, that runs beside the waterfront with several willow trees stretching over the trail. As he walks, he reflects on the times he spent in Kitzingen. Up ahead, there are benches and a playground with a small boat built for kids to play upon to the left.

Rick continues his stroll by the river, enjoying the gorgeous day with the trees in full bloom. May is always a good time to be in Germany. All the houses have traditional flower boxes hanging on the window ledges. The wind is blowing gently. Enough to spread the scent of the flowers but not enough to distract from the sunny day along the Main River. Up ahead, poles along the way have flower fixtures of petunias attached to the poles. Every step lets you know that it is springtime in Germany.

Rick continues to the Old Bridge on the Main River. The over 700-year-old bridge crosses the river up ahead. To the left, the houses are of a traditional German sense; some are yellow, while others are orange, with one or two white. All have the old-style German roofing with windows peering over the Main River. The half-timbered houses are almost out of a fairytale.

Three distinct fragrances circulating in the air that catch Rick's attention. He noticed the first aroma when his walk first began. The flowers in almost every home's windowsill are in full bloom and create an energetic atmosphere with their floral scents. The second fragrance comes from a German bakery. The unmistakable smell of freshly baked bread is a thing of beauty. Not only does it soothe the nose, but it also tempts the stomach. The third fragrance is the smell of perfume that he has grown to love. The scent of Poison is something that the love of his life has worn for just those special occasions. It is an unmistaken fragrance. Once you have had the pleasure of the aroma of Poison perfume around, you will never forget it.

Rick looks over at one of the benches, and there sits a lady with brown hair in a pixie cut. Her short hair flows with the breeze. Rick walks closer to her as she slowly smiles. He recognizes this smile; it is a smile that people want to be around. Her smile is mesmerizing to Rick. It is infectious. He knows this woman. Yep, it is Katja, the woman he has given his heart to. Not only is her smile infectious but one gets lost in her brown eyes. One glance into those eyes, and the song ♪ *Brown Eyed Girl* ♪ fills your head. She is a woman who is physically fit and is about 5 foot 6 that have curves that complement her.

"Hey stranger, don't let my husband see you talking to me. You know he is a jealous man," Katja says as she looks at Rick.

"I'll take my chances," he replies in all sincerity.

Katja gives Rick a quick look over from head to toe and pauses on his lips.

"So handsome guy, what brings you here?" She says in a seductive tone.

"I'm just looking for easy women," he replies with a shrug. "Some people told me to come down to the river and you will always find one."

Katja stands up and kisses Rick. Then she slowly moves her mouth away from his and whispers into his ear, "now, who told you about us easy women, hm? How did that get out when I was trying to keep it on the down-low?"

Rick's mouth curls into a smile. "People talk, Katja, people talk. I see you got a reputation to uphold."

Katja looks Rick in the eyes flirtatiously. "Well, since I am so easy, the least you can do is take an easy girl out for a meal first."

"Hungry, are we?" Rick asks with a smirk then replies, "but of course, my love."

Katja looks at Rick with a sincere expression and says, "Rick even though I have fantasies about wild guys and unknown men, you're the only guy I want in me."

He gives her a quick, conforming kiss then offers his arm.

Katja graciously loops her arm with his and they start walking towards the Old Bridge.

"Rick, let's walk part of the bridge first since it's such a lovely day," Katja directs Rick.

The pair walks up the staircase along the bridge and starts moving away from the main town towards the eastern part of Kitzingen. Halfway across, they stop at the memorial on the south side of the bridge. The memorial is meant to remind people not to forget about those missing in action in any war.

Katja reflects and asks, "Rick how many times have we met someone at this exact spot?"

Rick smiles and replies, "more than I can remember."

Rick points to the island in the middle of the river and turns to Katja

"Remember when our kids would run over to the public swimming pool on that island? Those were good times."

A smile comes across Katja's face, and she starts laughing. "They would pull their swim trunks down when going down the big slide so they could go faster."

Rick shakes his head with a chuckle.

"Oh, the memories of this town were incredible, don't you think, Rick?" Katja asks.

"I do, Katja," Rick professes.

"Rick, why don't we walk down to the statue of the lady that points at us before we get something to eat? If you have time like that for an easy lady," Katja says flirtatiously.

"Katja, easy women are not supposed to be this much work, I'm just saying," Rick said. Katja smiles.

The couple starts their walk back into the old part of town, passing a Café by the bridge corner on their right and crossing into the center of town. The strong scent of fresh Brötchen lingers in the air as they pass by a bakery on their left. The city fountain is nestled in the middle of a few restaurants and shopping stores and serves as a gathering point for the locals.

Rick and Katja continue to walk along the old cobblestone street that has been there for centuries. Who knows how many generations have walked this same path? Old houses border each side of the road along the route. Several of the homes are older than the United States itself. Each home is aligned like row houses but with an older feel. Up ahead, the famous Leaning Tower can be spotted, with its unique tilt gracing the top. English ivy reaches almost halfway up the tower. At the bottom and to the left of the tower, sits a statue of a wine keg standing on its end with a lady wearing a jester's hat pointing towards something. This was their destination to reminisce for a bit.

Rick and Katja share a few "remember this, remember that, and so on's."

Rick grabs up Katja and they dance around between the tower's base and the so called "pointing lady." Simply just enjoying the time as they reminisce. They abruptly come to a stop with a passionate kiss. Their lips locked together with love as a moment of stillness comes over them, and they slowly break away from the kiss.

Katja breaks the silence and smiles. "Let's get something to eat."

They walk back to the fountain and sit down at a restaurant that serves ice cream. An excellent place, it overlooks the activities of the few shops around the fountain. Instead of a big meal, they order some Spaghetti Eis, a local ice cream favorite. Katja orders one with the taste of raspberries, and Rick orders one with chocolate. They take their time eating and just enjoying the scenery of a lovely little German town.

Katja leans over to Rick and dips her spoon into Rick's ice cream and steals a scoop from him. She smiles as she eats the ice cream.

Rick shakes his head and says, "it seems some things never change, my love."

Katja grins and says, "no, they don't. Would you expect anything different from me?"

Rick chuckles, "no, not at all. I wouldn't have it any other way."

GETTING HIRED

Katja and Rick sit by the fountain simply embracing the ambiance of southern Germany. People pass by as they listen to the water pour from the fountain. Freshly baked bread is placed into some small containers by the baker, getting ready to be shipped out to convenience stores while the loaves are still fresh and warm. A local Imbiss is heating their tasty delicacy on the vertical rotisserie down the street. An older man is buying a small bouquet of flowers, most likely for his wife. He smells them before leaving the store. A lady strolls the usual cobblestone path that she has taken for years. The small town is vibrant with life but at a comfortable, slow pace.

Katja turns away from the happenings and looks at Rick.

"Let's go back to where our lives changed forever, you know the place, my love."

Rick turned toward Katja. "Okay, let's do it," he said with a nod.

Katja and Rick stroll towards the small inn that they stayed at on their first night in Kitzingen. The ole Gasthaus is on the west side of the train tracks and has a little restaurant downstairs. The restaurant serves traditional hearty German dishes such as Schnitzel or Bratwurst. This quaint little eatery is where Katja and Rick met Franz for the first time.

That first evening in Kitzingen, Katja and Rick had flown into Europe with their children from Fort Bliss, Texas. They arrived that evening at the Gasthaus where they would stay for about a week until they received adequate quarters. Together they had been married for some time and had come to Kitzingen as a blended family. Rick had three children from a previous marriage, Michael, Jonas, and Emma. At the same time, Katja had Noah. The couple had a son between them named Sebastian. That first evening at the Gasthaus, they had just finished their nice German meal and sent the kids upstairs to one of the two rooms they had reserved to settle down for the evening.

Rick and Katja remain sitting at their table to finish their meal. A man approaches the table wearing traditional Bavarian clothing. He had a nice wool jacket over a red and white checkered buttoned-up shirt. The man had on brown Lederhosen that went right below the knee and wool socks that went above the calf but left about an inch of bare skin between the socks and the Lederhosen. His hair was black and slightly silver, and his stature was around six feet tall.

"Hallo, my name is Franz." He spoke with a thick Bavarian accent. "May I have a moment of your time?"

Katja looked up at the stranger and kindly replied, "Sure, my name is Katja, and this is my husband, Rick."

"Yes, this I know. I know who you both are," Franz replied.

Rick and Katja looked at each other, sincerely puzzled, and almost simultaneously replied, "what?"

"Yes, I have a file on both you and your military service. I can tell you all about you and your children," Franz stated.

Rick stood up, protectively stepped toward Franz.

"What the hell is going on here?"

Franz put his hand on Rick's chest reassuringly and said, "there is nothing to be alarmed about, but this conversation would be better someplace quiet. Might I suggest your second room, or we take a stroll down by the river, just us three? I give you my word no one is in danger." Franz glances upstairs and says, "they are safe too."

Katja feeling worried, interjected, "let's go upstairs now. I want to see my kids."

As they got upstairs one of the doors was open. Katja quickly ran in. She finds a young lady in her late 20s sitting there with the kids.

The oldest of the five Taylor kids, Michael, turned to Katja as she walked up to the group. "Hey Mom, this is Sabine, and she said she is going to be our babysitter." Michael smiled at his mom sheepishly. Sabine was tall with flowing blonde hair that reached down to the middle of her back. She was beautiful and Michael liked that about her. Katja looked at Rick and Franz in bewilderment.

Franz then interjected. "Well, Michael, that is if, your mom and dad agree. See Katja; they are in good hands, I assure you. Why don't we have a stroll down by the river?" Katja confusingly nods yes, and Rick is still speechless. Franz turns to Sabine.

"Can you ensure the children are bedded down before 9 p.m. and stay with them until Katja and Rick return?"

"I would be glad to," Sabine said with a smile.

"Oh, wait." Franz halts. "Just to put everyone at ease here, I want to give you your own cell phone, Katja and Rick. In there is Sabine's number. Go ahead, one of you, give her a call."

Katja flips the phone open and sees a few numbers already programmed into the phone, including one labeled with Rick's name. She scrolls down to Sabine and gives it a ring. Sabine's phone buzzes.

Sabine answers, "Ja. Hallo, Katja."

"I think it is time for me to get Rick and Katja up to speed on everything. Sabine, we will be back within the hour," Franz informs everyone.

Rick, Katja, and Franz walk out the door and head towards the center of town and the river. As they got down by the river, Franz looked around to ensure no one else was present.

"Ok, Rick and Katja, let me explain what is going on."

Franz stops by some steps that lead into the Main River. "Let us all sit down."

The group takes a seat on the river steps.

"As I told you, my name is Franz. I work for the Agency," Franz explains. "I will not tell you which Agency, but I will tell you it is from America, and the Agency will always do what is good for America."

Rick and Katja listen intently to the information Franz tells them, trying to decide if they should believe what he is saying or not.

"We have been watching both of you for some time," Franz continues. "The Agency would like to offer you both a position that would not interfere with your military duties. Rather, it would complement them."

Rick is shocked by this proposition. Could this Agency be a secret part of the government? How do they not know about this? Would it really not interfere with their duties?

Katja is perplexed by all the information she is hearing. How would this not interfere with the Army?

"As you move throughout your military career, there will be times when we call upon you at your locations, asking you to do other work for the Agency," Franz tells them. "Such as, while you are in Kitzingen, it could be retrieving a packet, spying on someone, and so forth. With this opportunity comes several things. Our time is limited, so I will spit a few things out. One is you have Sabine as a permanent babysitter, or as some may call them, a nanny. She is part of the Agency as well. Your children will be protected and nurtured in a way like never before. She will have knowledge about all your missions to ensure everyone is on the same sheet of music."

Franz pauses for a moment to ensure Rick and Katja understand and then proceeds. "You will be paid through an account in Switzerland that is slowly routed to your account, which will not raise any red flags. The IRS will never be an issue, for we have cleared that avenue. However, other people or groups may try to search you and your financials will come up oblivious to them. From the outside, your finances will look like a typical Soldiers account. You will receive pay at such a rate that you and your children will never have to worry about money. Speaking of taking care of everything, your brother, Ben."

"Wait, what do you know about Ben?" Rick asks.

Franz looks at Rick reassuringly and says, "Rick, I know everything about you, my friend. We will make sure Ben gets the best care there is and that he is in the best facility available. You will only need to be the brother that loves and visits him. No financial burden will be yours."

Rick and Katja look at each other in a little disbelief. They look back at Franz and he replies, "we can move him within a couple of days to the care facility of your choosing, you just have to say the word. The Agency will take care of all his medical and financial needs that he will ever incur. That won't be your problem anymore, Rick."

Rick's anxiety begins to simmer down some.

Franz continues, "We have already found you a house to live in here in Kitzingen. Inside of it, there are a few things that will be at your disposal. There is 50 thousand euros in cash to be used as needed for call-up missions. There is also a passport in German for each of you and a different American passport. All with different aliases. Finally, several M9 Berettas with silencers are placed in several small gun safes throughout the house."

"Wait, what?" interjected Katja. "You said guns?"

"Yes, Katja, we know you had guns in the house under lock-in key in America, and we realize you are both quite familiar with the Beretta, so we thought the Beretta would be comfortable for both of you," Franz assured. "Now, we have a gun safe under each side of the bed; both have a right-handed keypad for the finger code. We have one under the tabletop on the computer desk and one under the couch in the living room. Each safe has the same code to alleviate any confusion."

"Stop everything," Rick interjects. "So, you're going to pay us for exactly what? You want us to be spies? Won't our kids be in danger?"

Franz looks at Rick. "I understand your concerns, Rick, I do, and you can turn us down. You will never hear from us again if you do, and this conversation practically never happened," Franz said. "But yes, we would like for you to be spies. The Agency believes you are the right people for the job. I will be your coordinator. Meaning I will send you both, along with Sabine, a note or message with instructions and you just follow the orders. Most missions will only take a few hours. If there are any mop-up issues, such as a death, inform me, and I have people for that."

This time, Katja interjects. "We are to kill people?"

"Most of the time, no," Franz responds. "You will gather intelligence or maybe steal something most of the time, but there are times you may have to kill someone. We ask is if you do kill someone, please do this behind closed doors and inform me immediately so I can get a mop-up team there quickly. You won't have to worry about the police. All you must do is say 'my lawyer is Franz.'"

"That's it, just say Franz?" Rick exclaims.

"Yes, Rick," Franz states. "Once my name is mentioned, it is put in the report. When it hits the computer, I am immediately notified, and I work with the law department behind the scenes, which you will be released."

"Look, my friends, we keep as much stress off you as possible," Franz says reassuringly. "Yes, you will have to spy, listen, acquire information, maybe steal, and even kill but everything else is covered. You will experience financial freedom for one. Second, you are already patriotic and support your country. You will just be adding another ingredient to that," Franz explains.

"How often should we expect to be on missions?" Katja asks.

"A few weeks out of the year to about a month out of the year is normally what happens," Franz responds. "Now, I will explain this to you. You may be going on vacation too, let's say, Greece. While there, at your evening meal, Rick may receive a text giving you some instructions for a mission later that evening. It may even be for both of you. You will have Sabine on all your vacations, so the children will not be an issue. She will know as well." Franz pauses and smiles, "with Sabine, you also have someone to take all your family photos for you while you are on vacation or wherever."

Katja and Rick look at each other briefly. Then Rick asks, "how long do we have to decide?"

"Until we return to the hotel," Franz responds.

"Do you mind if Katja and I just talk for a moment?"

"No problem, I will go down to the bridge and have a smoke; I'll be back after my cigar, if that is alright?" Franz confirms.

After Franz is out of earshot, Rick and Katja go over the proposal.

Katja looks at Rick. "What do you think? Is this us?" she asks.

Rick replies, "this is crazy, Katja, we haven't been here a full day, and we are offered to be spies out of nowhere. Am I hallucinating?"

Katja shakes her head. "No, Rick, I just heard the same thing. Who would have ever thought this would happen? I guess the idea that we are good at our jobs may have tipped them off. I do not know how else they found us. Or could it have been one of our past leaders suggested to us?"

Rick thinks momentarily. "We had that one officer that used to be with the CIA. Do you think it could have been him?"

"Who knows, Rick, but we have a decision to make right now. What do you think, my love?" she asks.

Rick looks down and ponders for a moment. He slowly lifts his head and grins.

"This is so cool. No one would ever believe us or understand this. Remember when we got married, we wanted to enjoy the adventure of life. Well, this is it, Katja. What do you think?"

Katja returns her husband's smile. "My love, I love it, but I worry about the kids."

"I do to on that, Katja," Rick replies.

Katja slowly gives a mischievous grin and exclaims, "We only live once, right?"

"Damn right, Katja," Rick says.

Franz blows out his last puff on his cigar and slowly strolls back to the couple. "Okay, guys, what do you think?"

"We're in!" Katja exclaims.

Rick gives an approving nod.

In an instructional manner, Franz begins. "Okay guys, so in your phones, there are several things that you need to review. If you lose your phone, notify me immediately so I can clear it." Franz gestures toward the phone still in Katja's hand.

"If you both open your phone, go to the icon on the lower left of the main screen, and click on that. That is your Swiss account. There has been deposited $150,000 in your account for each of you. You will both receive that annually. In the morning, check your accounts, and $8,000 will be transferred from the Swiss account to your current personal account. You can do that at will, but I ask you to never transfer more than $8,000 at a time. That causes me to do a lot of work when you do that."

Franz pauses to make sure the couple is still following before he continues.

"In your phone is my number, Sabine's number, each of your numbers, and a number listed under töten, which means kill. When you dial the töten number, that means there is a problem with the mission. You don't have to talk. Just dial it. After the first ring, we will know there is an issue. Inside your phone there is also a GPS, so we know where you are. Do you have any questions?"

"Yes, when is our first mission?" Rick eagerly asks.

Franz smiles. "That's my boy. I like that, and I see we are eager. Your first mission will be in a few weeks. I will reach out to you a couple of times a week for the first three weeks, just to get you ready for anything."

Katja nods in an accepting way as she takes in everything.

Franz then stretches out his arms in a guiding way. "My friends, let us make our way back if you would. We can talk about my relationship with you along the way back but let us not talk about the Agency. There could be ears around."

Rick and Katja start heading back to the Gasthaus with Franz.

Katja asks, "so, what is our relationship?"

"I am your guide the entire time you are with us. I will be your best friend. Think of me as your coordinator or orchestrator," Franz replies.

Franz pauses for a moment. "Now, when we return, Sabine is your nanny as far as your children know. But she is very skilled in martial arts and weaponry as well. She will be both nanny and protector. The kids only need to know about the nanny part. Tomorrow, the military will say you need to go to the Housing Referral Office to get on the housing list. Once they type your name in on the computer, your house will magically pop up and be available strictly for your family. That will go through the military on that part. They will be unaware of the arrangements we have already made, but you will be able to move in, in about two days. They will offer you military furniture until your furniture arrives, but I ask you to keep the sofa, your bed, and the computer table in the house. They are prepared for you. The computer desk has a secondary safe with your passports and mission money. I will text you one code for all safes when you step into the house. Do you have any questions?"

"None right now, just a lot to take in," Rick says with an exhausted chuckle.

"I think I need a glass of wine to let this all settle in. I do have one question," Katja announces. "Is this real? I mean, seriously, is this real? We were in America just 24 hours ago and now we have more than we bargained for."

Franz smiles. "I assure you that this is real, and we are lucky to have you guys."

Reaching the front of the Gasthaus, Rick and Katja walk in with Franz following. As they get upstairs to their room, the door opens, and Sabine comes out. Her long blonde hair bounces around, at times in her tan face, and she says, "oh, they are so precious. I think the plane ride wore them out. They are all asleep. I will tell you that they are very inquisitive, especially little Emma."

Franz looks at Sabine and says, "well, Sabine, you have a new family."

Sabine smiles and claps quietly, saying, "yes, yes!" Sabine then gives Katja a big hug and hugs Rick as well. "Oh, we will have so much fun, I promise you guys," Sabine exclaims.

THE FIRST MISSION NOTIFICATION

*O*ver the next few weeks, Katja and Rick began working at Harvey Barracks on the east side of Kitzingen. It was a nice small military Kaserne with an airfield, though there was not much on the Kaserne but a few Battalions and a Brigade Headquarters. There was also a Burger King and a Cantina on the post for the troops if they didn't want to eat in the Chow Hall. Their perspective duties allowed Katja to get home earlier than Rick. Their house was nestled a few minutes' walk from the west side of the Main River and a few minutes' walk from the center of town.

It is a Friday afternoon around 5:30 pm as Katja arrives home. She opens the door, and Sabine immediately greets her.

"The kids have been wonderful. Michael is downstairs listening to music. Noah and Jonas are playing. Emma is coloring, and little Sebastian is taking a nap," Sabine smiles. "So, how was your day?"

Katja breathes out heavily. "Oh, I am so glad the week is over, and it is time for the weekend. I want to relax."

"I understand. I do," Sabine says sweetly. "Oh, guess what. I have coffee ready for you."

Katja smiles and hugs Sabine. "Thank you so much. You have been a Godsend. We are fortunate to have you."

Sabine puts her hand on her heart and tilts her head to the left and down with a soft "thank you." Katja and Sabine go into the living room and sit down to have coffee and cake.

"So, how long have you been doing this?" Katja asks, making polite conversation.

"Well, you are my second family," Sabine shares.

Katja takes a sip of the coffee and is pleasantly surprised. While looking at Sabine, Katja replies, "Oh my this is the best cup of coffee I have had in some time. What kind is this?"

Sabine replies, "Katja, my dear, you have been in America too long. It is Jacob's coffee."

Katja smiles and says, "no way, it's been a long time." Katja takes another sip. "So, what happened to your first family?" She inquires.

Sabine slowly takes a sip and replies, "well, they got out of the business."

Katja and Sabine's phones both vibrate. Katja looks down, and it shows that it is a message from Franz. She clicks on the text to find one word written - "Mission."

She looks up at Sabine, and Sabine is smiling at her.

"Oh, I'm so excited for you," she says happily. "You are going to do well."

She leans over and gives Katja a reassuring hug.

Rick just arrived home and walked through the door.

"Hey Katja, I got something on the phone."

Katja replies, "yes, we know."

Bewildered, Rick asks, "who is we?"

"Oh, I am, we," Sabine says with a laugh.

"Oh, okay, I got it," Rick says. "So, what is next?"

"Well, open the message fully, and all the details will be there." Sabine says, then pauses for a moment before continuing. "I think the kids and I will watch a movie tonight while you two are out having a good time."

Rick turns to Sabine graciously, "thank you, Sabine."

Sabine snaps and waves her hands downward. "Oh, stop it and go get ready."

Katja and Rick go into their bedroom and look at their phones regarding the message. They then look at each other, and Katja says, "are you ready my love?" Rick smiles. They click on the message, and it reads:

Katja and Rick, today's mission is easy. You are to retrieve a cell phone from Kristoff Fischer. He is around 6 foot 1, has a tan complexion, brown hair, and brown eyes. He always wears a dinner coat and typically keeps the phone in his right pocket. He likes to eat at the Café by the bridge corner. Kristoff enjoys flicking his zippo while sitting down at the table. He likes to eat at the table close to the bar normally. Kristoff is there every Friday evening, starting around 8 pm. He prefers to pick up on any lady who looks alone in the bar. Kristoff will generally take them to a Gasthaus close by, down the river about 200 yards, and spend the night with them. You are to get the phone, and he is not to be hurt or killed.

Katja gasps as she looks at Rick. "Oh my gosh, will I have to sleep with this guy?"

Rick looks in disbelief and shakes his head sideways. "Surely not," he replies.

"Rick!" Katja loudly exclaims. "Rick, that implies I may have to."

Katja's voice carries throughout the house.

Rick replies, "I don't know, Katja. I really don't know, but I do not like that if it is the case."

Sabine then interrupts the conversation by entering the room.

"Guys, first of all, you do whatever it takes to get the mission complete. You must remember that," she says sternly. "But this will be an easy mission. Katja, this should not have to make it as far as the Gasthaus. Let us do some planning on this. We have an hour or so. You guys are okay, right?" Sabine nods her head up and down, hoping to calm them down.

Katja nervously nods back in acknowledgment.

"Okay, let's plan it out," Rick decides.

"But remember," Sabine restates. "No matter what you have to do to accomplish the mission, you do it even if it means sleeping with someone for the night. Whatever it takes, you do it, do you understand?"

Rick looks at Sabine and says, "can you give us a moment."

Sabine replies, "certainly," and walks out of the room.

"Rick! Rick, what are we doing honey?" Katja exclaims in an almost pleading way.

"Katja, this is living life on the edge. We can make it through this. We are way stronger than this don't you think?" Rick asks, looking for reassurance.

"Yes, we are," Katja assures him and then says, "so we are both good with this, right?"

"Of course, my love." Rick replies.

They kiss each other intimately, until Katja breaks the kiss and looks up at Rick with tears streaming down her cheek.

"You are my soul mate, and we will never break that, my love."

Rick kisses her again and then says, "Okay, let's do this. Come on, Sabine we got plans to make on this one."

As Sabine, Katja and Rick set up the plans for the first mission, Rick's mind drifts back to Katja possibly being intimate with another man. He asks himself; how far will this go?

What if the guy touches her in ways that only I have touched her for several years? He thinks. *What if the guy runs his hands over her body, skin to skin, or even has sex with her?*

The thought starts to anger him, and it does begin to bother him. There is no need to try to deny it. But he also feels that this keeps them alive as well. One thing is sure, he trusts Katja to do whatever it takes but also to make the best of each situation. There is a thin grey line which he can see either one of them having to cross from time to time. What happens if he has to sleep with a woman for the mission? Rick smiles internally.

Well, that wouldn't be so bad. All for the country, right? He mentally agrees with himself. He then considers what Katja would think about that. *Katja would kill that woman without blinking an eye*, he thinks to himself with a grin.

Sabine looks over, "Rick, do you got this?"

Rick snaps back into the planning and replies, "yes, I got it."

He looks over at Katja as she studies a map of the city.

Katja, as she stares at the map, is in her own thoughts as well.

What if Kristoff takes me to the Gasthaus? I cannot blow my cover for the sake of staying monogamistic. Katja ruminates to herself for a moment. *Rick has been the only person to kiss me or be intimate with me for a long time.*

It has been almost a decade since another man had touched her. It would be something so foreign to her at this point. *Not that I would be betraying Rick because he understands the mission, but it would be something relatively novel to me.* It could be fresh and different. She knows it would only be temporary if something happened. Would Rick think less of her if the mission got sexual? Katja ponders that would be the worst of any outcome. Disappointing Rick or hurting him.

If the moment comes, Katja tells herself, *I will embrace the moment and make the most of it but keep the mission outcome in the forefront of my mind.* Before she could finish her resolve, another thought comes to her mind. *What if Rick sleeps with a woman on a mission?* Katja thinks to herself but soon finds comfort in her next thought. She won't hold that against Rick, for it is part of the job. *But I will definitely kill that bitch.*

THE MISSION AT THE CAFÉ
BY THE BRIDGE CORNER

Katja confidently walks into the Café by the bridge corner around 7:45 pm wearing a pair of leopard spot high waisted velvet pants and a red silk blouse with the top two buttons undone and part of her stomach showing. As she walked in the door, every head in Café turned to examine her. Men and women alike look over at Katja. Young, old, and middle-aged all had to survey this woman entering the bar. One woman even licked her lips with a yearning, or maybe it was a simple admiration of Katja walking into the bar with no fear. Katja's brown pixie cut hair looks very European and compliments her attire. She walks up to the bar and sits down for a second. Behind the bar is a mirror that allows her to see the tables behind her.

The bartender approaches her, and before he can get a word out, Katja raises her index finger and thumb and says, "two vodkas please."

The bartender asks, "do you want the good or cheap stuff?"

"It doesn't matter," Katja replies as she puts a 20 euro on the bar.

The bartender gives the nod and starts working on the two shots. He happens to be shorter than Katja and is sporting a buttoned-up black shirt with the top button unbuttoned and black slacks. His attire complements his short black hair. Almost like a soldier's haircut except the top goes in various directions. He is wearing a nice gold watch and no rings. It is quite apparent that the bartender is conscious of his appearance.

Katja glances around the room and realizes most of the men are still staring at her. There is no sign of Kristoff, but it is still early.

The bartender returns with a smile. "Two vodkas," he says, setting the shots down in front of Katja.

The door opens to the bar, and a gentleman in a dark blue blazer walks in wearing tan khakis and a light blue shirt. He is tall, with a dark tan, brown hair, brown eyes, and his shirt's top two buttons left undone to be sexy. The man looks to be in his early 30s and is quite good-looking. The gentleman nods his head towards the bartender. The bartender nods back and responds with a Bavarian accent, "Hallo, Kristoff."

Inside, Katja's stomach started having butterflies from the anticipation.

Is this the man who will touch me? Or kiss me? Katja is very nervous.

Kristoff says in his own Bavarian accent, "the usual if you don't mind, Max." Kristoff seems quite comfortable in the Café, almost as if this is his second home or that he has some propriety rights to the place.

Katja picked up that the bartender was named Max. She sits there for a bit, extremely nervous and looking into her shots that she had not drunk yet. Behind her, she hears a noise. She looks in the mirror, and Kristoff sits at his table, flicking his Zippo open and close. He eventually pulls out a cigarette and starts to light it.

Here goes nothing, Katja thinks to herself.

She quickly downs both vodkas, turns around and walks to Kristoff's table. She looks him in his brown eyes, and flirtatiously asks, "do you have one of those for me?"

Kristoff seems pleasantly surprised but pulls out another cigarette. "But of course," he exclaims with an eager smile.

Katja notices it is a Haus Bergmann cigarette. A popular German brand.

Katja blows Kristoff a pretend kiss and puts the cigarette in her mouth as he confidently lights it for her. She notices that his fingernails are perfectly manicured, and she can still smell his cologne over the strong cigarette smell. She then winks at him, leans to where her mouth is next to his ear.

"I think you're cute," Katja whispers in his ear, then pulls away and makes a sensual walk to the bathroom with the cigarette in her left hand.

When she gets into the bathroom, she steps into a stall and quickly shuts the stall door. Katja breathes out heavily. She takes a deep drag off the cigarette to calm her nerves. Katja contemplates if this will be the night that someone else kisses her. How far will this go, she wonders. After a few puffs, Katja finishes the cigarette. She opens the stall door and looks into the mirror to prepare for her return.

As she walks back into the room, Katja notices Kristoff has a Hefe Weizen beer and French Fries. She walks by his table, grabs one of his fries, dips it in the mayonnaise. Gradually she puts the mayonnaise-soaked fry in her mouth as she looks at Kristoff, then winks at him flirtatiously.

Kristoff is completely stunned by this. He looks a little lost and a little overwhelmed at the same time. It appears Kristoff is not used to someone else being in charge of the situation. At this moment, Katja is calling all the shots.

She looks at Max, who is wiping his bar, and says, "another vodka."

All this entertains Max. He is smiling and trying not to laugh as he brings her one immediately.

Kristoff comes up to Katja and asks, "would you like to accompany me?"

Katja smiles and responds wittingly, "I thought you would never ask."

Katja knows she has him hooked, and he is like putty in her hands.

Wow, most men would not be that excited until at least a kiss, but if it works, then it works, she thinks.

Now she just hopes the rest of the plan works out. She brings her shot glass to the table and watches Kristoff take a big drink from his tall Weizen glass. Without asking, she takes a couple more of his fries.

"My name is Kristoff," he tells Katja. "Are you an American here?"

"I guess you could say that," Katja responds. "My name is Katja. I work on the base." Kristoff starts eating another fry when Katja says, "I said you were cute so why are we staying around here, tripping over pleasantries when maybe we could go somewhere quiet."

Kristoff chokes on his food for a second. Then he chugs a big drink from the Weizen glass, tosses 30 euros on the table, and waves at Max. "This is for the lady and me."

Max nods in approval and smiles mischievously.

Katja grabs Kristoff's arm and whispers to him, "do you know a place we can go?"

"Yes, I have a place that I keep on Fridays and Saturdays just a little further down by the river," Kristoff says.

Katja gives him a flirtatious smile. "Nice. I would like a stroll down by the river as we go to your place."

Kristoff is feeling pretty lucky about the evening, and they walk out the door onto the cobblestone street and take a left to head to the river.

The evening has turned dark as they walk past the bridge. Kristoff and Katja head south along the river, with Kristoff closest to the river and his right arm intertwined with Katja's.

In the dark along the river, a jogger can be seen heading their way. Kristoff is looking at Katja, sweet talking her as they stroll down by the riverside. The jogger is getting closer and picks up speed.

Kristoff finally notices the jogger out of the corner of his eye and yells, "watch out."

Katja covertly reaches into his right pocket and retrieves his phone.

The jogger then knocks Kristoff into the river. As he resurfaces in the river, Katja flees the scene immediately, and the jogger continues to run.

Katja runs at a good sprint for about 1/4 of a mile before she finally slows down to a jog. Her heart is racing, not from the sprint, but from the events that transpired.

A few minutes later, Katja links up with the jogger, who happens to be Rick, on the street where they live. They pull each other into a tight hug as both their hearts are pounding. They grab each other's hands and skip back to their house. As they get closer to their home, they can see a silhouette in their front yard smoking a cigar. They approach cautiously and realize it is Franz. A sigh of relief comes over them. The aroma of Franz's cigar takes over all senses.

"Hallo, my friends. It seems to be a pleasant evening, don't you think," Franz says.

"Franz, it is so good to see you," Katja replies with a smile.

"Do you have something for me?" Franz asks. "If so, let's be quiet about it, and go inside the basement."

The three of them walk into the house and proceed to the basement. Once they all get down there, they shut the door.

Once the door is closed, Katja hands over the cell phone that was taken from Kristoff, Franz smiles.

"Ah yes, this we will investigate deeply," Franz says. "Good job, guys. So, do you guys have any questions?"

Rick instantly asks in a stern voice, "yes, how far do we have to go for the mission? Are we expected to sleep with people to make these things happen?"

Katja was listening eagerly to Rick's questions.

"Yes," Franz informed. "Whatever it takes to get it done, you need to do it. You are a strong couple and understand that there are no feelings between you and your, how do I say, hmmm, victims. So, please don't make it about emotion, that doesn't mean you don't have fun with the mission, but I must explain this, and you need to listen carefully. Sabine's previous family was also a husband-and-wife team. They had the mission of retrieving a floppy disk from the guy. They agreed that she would go to the hotel, deceive the guy, and run off with the floppy disk. In the mission orders, we stated it was okay to kill him. This couple decided they didn't want to do that, nor did she want to sleep with the guy. So, the husband stayed out of the scene completely. The wife went to the hotel, and as the guy went to the restroom, she retrieved the floppy disk and tried to leave. The guy came out of the bathroom, caught her, and killed her. We had a camera in that hotel room because it was used often. So, we were able to analyze it. The husband understandably left the Agency. That is why Sabine didn't have a family to work with anymore. That is also why it is important to understand that you do the mission at all costs. I hope you two understand that."

Katja and Rick were both in shock but nodded their heads, understanding and agreeing with it.

"Well, let's not dwell on past mistakes," Franz says. "I think it's time for a toast, so let's go upstairs and celebrate with Sabine. How does that sound?"

"Hell yeah!" Katja responds. "I am starving and need a drink."

Later that night, Rick and Katja embraced each other intimately in a way that they had not done so since their wedding night.

"Rick, this was so exhilarating tonight!" Katja blurts out when they take a break in the action.

"Well, you're welcome, my love," Rick replied.

"No, not that," Katja says, and then she laughs as Rick flirtingly gives a surprising look. "I mean the mission tonight; I was so nervous and grateful that my friendly secret jogging lover came through."

"Wait, you have a secret lover, my dear?" Rick questions jokingly.

Katja sheepishly says, "well, I have been trying to keep that a secret, my love, but he does do things you don't do to me. I hope you understand."

Rick gasps in an exaggerated sense. "Uh, I try my best, my love."

Katja sympathetically says, "I know, I know, but you're the one I love, my Rick."

Katja leans over and rubs him over his underwear, picking back up where they had left off.

CHILDREN AND THEIR GAMES

A typical day at the Taylor home has Rick and Katja at work, and in the summertime, the kids are at home with Sabine. Each one of the kids is unique. Michael is the oldest at 17 years of age. He has blond hair, blue eyes and is about 5 foot 11, just an inch shorter than Rick. He likes skateboarding, girls, and participating in mischief. Next in age are Jonas and Emma, the twins. They are 15 years of age; both with blond hair and blue eyes. Jonas is a brilliant kid with a more petite frame of about 5 foot 8 and is into being witty, girls, hanging out with the local German kids, and of course, his own misbehavior. At the same time, Emma is considered tall for a girl. She is 5 foot 10. Emma likes boys, but she also likes the bakery and sometimes acquires extra things from the store without paying for them. She is very street savvy. Noah is 14 years old; he is 5 foot 9, and he has a dark complexion, dark hair, and brown eyes. He likes girls, hanging out with local German kids, is very street-savvy, and is into some shenanigans. Then there is Sebastian, who is 4 feet tall with brown eyes and blond hair. He is 10 years old and still finding his way. The rest of the children protect him a lot. He is into Legos, football, and just hanging out. They all take advantage of swimming in the public pool during the summer break.

The Taylor house is very accommodating. It is a five-bedroom, two-bathroom house. The house consists of three stories and has a large game room in the basement. Like most German homes, the floors are all heated. It sits right off the street with an alley that leads to three other houses.

Michael has a room downstairs in the basement, and across from him is a rather large room used as a game room. Because there isn't a restroom downstairs, Michael goes to the first floor to use the restroom, which also has a shower. Noah and Jonas share a room on the second floor. Emma has her own room on the second floor, and Sabine has her room on the second floor. There is a bathroom on the second floor that everyone uses except for Sabine and Michael to help keep the congestion down. Katja and Rick have their bedroom on the 3rd floor. There is also a living room, a dining room, and a coat entrance that connects to that restroom all on the first floor.

Sabine is a beautiful young lady who is 28 years of age. She weighs about 115 pounds and is 5 foot 8. Sabine has long, wavy blonde hair that hangs over her shoulders and to the middle of her back. Her figure is entirely complimentary. Sabine's eyes are blue. Michael, Noah, and Jonas have grown fond as teenagers of eyeballing her often. Sabine has handled this quite maturely.

One Thursday, Katja and Rick left for work early in the morning. Sabine takes her morning shower before everyone else gets up. This usually is her quiet time. Michael, Noah, and Jonas sneak up to the bathroom as she takes a shower. The bathroom door has a window above it, common in German houses. The boys lift each other to peek in as Sabine is showering, one at a time.

Noah giggles frantically as the steam rises along with the window.

Jonas tells Noah, "Shush before we get caught."

Michael peaks up there too. He can see Sabine naked.

Noah giggles and exclaims, "I can see her boobies."

Jonas laughs as they all gaze at Sabine naked in the shower.

Suddenly, the shower turns off, and Sabine opens the bathroom door and walks out completely naked. Water is still dripping off her perfectly sculpted body. The boys are in shock and mesmerized. All they can see is a naked woman in front of them. They can see her boobies. They can see her hair perfectly manicured below her waistline that covers her vagina. Sabine's voice breaks the deafening silence as she asks, "Is this what you wanted to see, boys?" Water is still dripping onto the floor. All three are speechless and turn red. "Stop! Do not go anywhere," she exclaims, "now look me in the eyes, and I want to tell you something."

Each boy slowly ashamedly lifts their head looking over her water-soaked body. Their eyes eventually make their way to Sabine's eyes. As they look eye to eye with Sabine, all three of their faces flush from embarrassment.

Sabine speaks very authoritatively. "Now, each of you has seen me, and trust me, there will be plenty of girls for you to look at, so let's make this the last time that it's me you're looking at." She raises her voice angrily for effect, "Do we understand each other, or do I need to talk to your parents?"

Michael immediately answers. "No, Ma'am, you don't need to talk to our parents."

Noah and Jonas shake their heads sideways rapidly to say no.

"Guys keep eye contact," Sabine directed, tilting her head to one side as she looked the boys in the eyes and said as she smiled, "how funny is it a naked girl stands here in front of you, and you just kept looking in her eyes."

She turned away and went back into the bathroom with a slow walk. Like nothing bothered her one bit. All three boys burst out laughing.

The boys aren't the only ones who can find themselves in a bit of trouble.

Emma would routinely walk downtown and go to the bakery or a candy store. Often, Emma could be seen running out of the store mainly because she would take more than she purchased. Little to her knowledge, the local shop owners adored her and didn't mind too much. But in her mind, she was getting over on them. Emma also gravitates to drama. Maybe that is just the teenager in her.

One afternoon Emma was looking out her window that faced the street. There were several boys riding their gas-powered scooters down the street. Sabine walked into her room and noticed this. She asked, "Emma, what are you up to?"

"Oh nothing, Sabine, just thinking about going outside," she replied.

Sabine came over to see what she was looking at. She looked at Emma and smiled. "You know that boy on the blue moped sure is cute."

Emma nodded. "He is. That is Phillip."

"So, you know his name?" Sabine asked.

"Oh, I know all their names," Emma said without a care. "That's Phillip, that's Finn, Tobias, and Klaus," she says as she points out each one.

Sabine is impressed with Emma's knowledge of the neighborhood kids.

Growing up with four brothers can be difficult, but Emma holds her own. At times she can be the brunt of jokes but one on one with her brothers she is not one to be taken lightly. Most of the time she would be in confrontation with either Noah or Jonas. Emma can defend herself quite well.

Noah and his local friend would often get caught purchasing smokes from the cigarette machine. Often, he would try to hide it, but routinely he would be caught in the act. In comparison, Jonas liked to embellish stories. Not necessarily lie, but instead, expand on the truth. On the other hand, Emma would lie quite a bit at times.

At times, the three oldest boys would swim across the Main River, which is over two football fields wide. As they would swim, there would often be large barges navigating the river. Each large barge brought with them a strong undertow. Michael, Noah, and Jonas were all solid swimmers, but they were not big people which they had to be in order to compete with that undertow.

Sebastian, being the smallest, would always be protected by the brothers and Emma. Attention around a house of five kids can be scarce at times, so each would posture for attention in their unique way.

A unique thing in the Taylor household was that each of the children also spoke German. Katja demanded it, and Sabine fully enforced it.

During the long days of the summer, Sabine, who is trained in a variety of fighting styles, would take them all out in the front yard and teach them martial arts in the morning. They would spend about three hours a day on this. Sabine would focus them on self-defense and how to bring a person down, a person that was bigger than them. She had a local friend, Markus, who was over six feet tall and weighed over 200 pounds that would come by about once a week so the kids could practice on someone dramatically larger than themselves. Each child, including Sebastian, had to flip Markus. Sabine focused the children on maximizing their speed and agility against aggressors and precise hit points to bring a larger person down. She was very disciplined in the approach and did not tolerate horseplaying during the training. Kids can have fun, but it was all business when it came to protecting themselves.

In the afternoon, they would all head to the local Swimming pool, to go swimming with their friends, and purchase ice cream or French Fries. While at the pool on the island in the Main River, they would link up with various local kids and head to the big spiral slide. As they would get to the top of the slide, they would have to wait until the lifeguard would give them the OK that the previous person was out of the way so they could slide. Once they got the OK, they would pull their swimming trunks down so they would be bare butt on the way down the slide. The kids had a theory that this would make them go faster, of course there was no conclusive evidence to say for sure. They would do this until they had to go back home, which would typically be around 4:00 p.m. Once arriving home, Sabine required that each clean their room while she prepared supper.

Yes, the children may have gotten a different education than most American children. They all received an education, lived in a different culture, and became quality neighbors, unlike some military brats who stayed in military housing and did not really blend in with the local people. They also expanded their physical prowess and their intellect.

One afternoon the kids are outside playing with the kids from the neighborhood. The boys are throwing a football in the street. Michael throws a beautiful pass through the air to Jonas.

A couple of local boys have their scooters and are riding around. Sabine walks outside and notices a scooter whizzing by with Phillip on the front of it and Emma riding on the back of it. Emma has her arms wrapped around Phillip and she is laughing as they go by. Sabine made a mental note of this.

Noah throws the football and Jonas runs in to Sebastian to catch it. Sebastian is knocked to the ground and starts crying. He is bleeding from his forehead. Sebastian notices the blood and his crying intensifies. Sabine immediately rushes over and scoops him up. She takes him into the house and to the bathroom. Michael, Noah, and Jonas follow immediately along with the rest of the neighborhood kids.

Michael gets a wash rag and runs water over it and hands it to Sabine. Sebastian is shaking and crying.

"Oh Sebastian, it's not as bad as it looks," Sabine says in a reassuring voice. "Tough guys bleed all the time. You just became a tough guy."

Sabine places the rag on his forehead to stop the bleeding.

Sebastian starts to calm down and the rest of the boys start to pump his ego a bit.

"Sebastian, dude that was a shot man" Noah says braggingly.

Next, Michael chimes in. "Wow, I would have been crying for Momma."

"Oh, it is a small cut," Sabine says. "You will have a little bruise but that is it."

Emma, who had just walked in asked "what happened?"

"You missed it as usual," Jonas says. "You out there flirting with Phillip."

"Shut up," Emma shouts as she shoves Jonas into the wall.

Sabine jumps in between the two siblings and says, "Emma why don't we go upstairs in a few and you can tell me about your scooter ride."

The boys all start chiming in with "oooh, you're in trouble now."

Sabine quickly turns to them and tells them firmly to "stop."

Immediately a pin drop could be heard. Emma walks upstairs to her room.

Sabine turns to Sebastian. "You're going to be fine, you will have a little scar there, don't bother it."

She starts walking upstairs, then stops to look back at Sebastian.

"Anyway, girls like guys with scars," she says with a slight wink.

The boys all start laughing.

When Sabine makes it to Emma's room, she finds her lying on her bed with her face buried in her pillow. Sabine sits down next to her and puts a gentle hand on her back.

"Emma," she says in a soft voice. "So, what is this deal with you on a moped with Phillip?"

"We were just riding," Emma replies.

"I realize this, but I also know that you think Phillip is cute. I can tell by the way you act," Sabine replied. "Every time he drives that scooter home you run to the window as soon as you hear him."

Emma lifts her head from her pillow and looks at Sabine in a shy fashion. "I do like him, he's fun."

"Emma," Sabine says in a serious tone. "There is nothing wrong with liking a boy, it is not anything to be ashamed of. You should be happy and proud to find him interesting. So, I don't want to ever see you embarrassed to talk about anyone you like. You understand?"

Emma smiles and Sabine gives her a big hug.

"Now Emma, tell me what you find interesting in this Mr. Phillip."

MISSION TWO

Kitzingen lies in a region of Germany known as Franconia, which is located in Bavaria. This Franconian region is famous for producing wine and is often called the Franconian Wine Country. The Main River bends back and forth through this region with one part of the river forming a distinct V known as the main triangle. Kitzingen lies near the bottom of this V. The river continues west to form more of a U, known as the main square. The small towns produce their wine throughout this region and each village has its perspective wine fest throughout the warmer months. This region is even famous for the shape of its wine bottles. The shape is an ellipsoid flattened with a neck attached to it. This bottle can only be used in the Franconia region and certain parts of Baden for Germany.

In a neighboring town of Iphofen, they are conducting their annual wine fest. Iphofen is southeast of Kitzingen with plenty of vineyards. It's a beautiful little Bavarian town with medieval towers throughout the city and a gatehouse that you can drive or walk through. Specifically, the gatehouse with a tall tower in town is famous. Tourists often make their way to this city to get their photos taken with the gatehouse. Cars can drive through it along the cobblestone street. There are various other towers within the city, as well. Some of the towers are built like a keep. While two other towers can be driven through by an opening at the bottom. Each of the towers in Iphofen were a formidable defense for the town in the past.

The center of town is where the wine fest is held. Often considered a grand celebration, the local townspeople dress up in their traditional Bavarian attire while enjoying the evening by singing traditional German songs and drinking fresh wine. There are tables strung out along the marketplace, each with the traditional orange tabletops and benchtops. A local band is playing traditional German songs, as well as a popular mix that even includes John Denver's ♪ *Take Me Home, Country Roads* ♪, which is a staple song played at almost every wine fest.

There may be nothing more unique than hearing Germans singing, ♪ *Country Roads* ♪ in a thick Bavarian accent.

Rick and Katja are enjoying the wine fest experience. Rick has already had one Bratwurst with a Brötchen, and Katja has had a couple of glasses of wine. The band plays a toast song about every three songs, and everyone is having a good time. Rick feels a vibration on his phone, and checks to see a text from Franz. Katja looks at her phone and sees the same text.

They nod to each other and go off to an out-of-the-way area to open the text.

Meet me outside the gatehouse in a few minutes.

The couple begin moving in that direction together with Katja still holding her wine glass.

"I'm taking my glass with me. It's a souvenir," she tells Rick.

He smiles at his wife when she stops abruptly. "Wait. Let me go get a refill before we go; Franz can wait a moment."

Rick just grins, shaking his head sideways.

As they approach the gatehouse, they see a familiar silhouette of a man smoking a cigar in the shadow of the opening to the gatehouse. The aroma from his cigar lingers in the air.

"Hallo, my friends, what a beautiful evening," Franz says.

"It is, we were having a good time," Rick replies. "So, do we have a mission tonight?"

"Let's walk outside the gatehouse down the street a bit. There are fewer ears around," Franz says as he puffs on the cigar. As they get a bit away from the town, Franz tells Katja and Rick why he contacted them. "No mission tonight, my friends, but I have to discuss an upcoming mission with you," says Franz. Rick and Katja look at Franz eagerly with anticipation. Franz turns to Katja with concern.

"Katja, you are not saying much tonight. Is everything ok?" he asks.

Katja laughs and then answers slowly, "Oh yes, just enjoying the smooth taste of this delicious wine."

Franz nods his head with a smile then returns to the matter at hand.

"So, when we dug into that phone you retrieved, Katja, we got a lot of information off it. We will have a mission soon for you to meet Hermann Krämer. He is a gentleman in his fifties. In Kristoff's phone, he was referred to often, along with a reference that the RAF is born again and is now called the Sharp Sickle. Do either of you know what the RAF is or means?" Franz asked.

Both Katja and Rick shook their heads, no and Rick responded. "Nope, never heard of it; wait, is that the Royal Air Force?"

Franz chuckled. "I guess it could be, but in this instance, they are referring to the Red Army Faction, a terrorist organization that started in the 60s and conducted bombings, assassinations, bank robberies and kidnappings of Americans and Germans here in Germany. They announced that they were dead in 1998, but they may have been revived, changed their name to Sharp Sickle, and we did not know it. I am a bit worried about this one because we do not have many details on this." Franz explains.

"Ok, so this is a little more difficult, right? We can handle that," Rick says reassuringly.

Franz quickly agrees. "I have no doubt that, but I must explain that this could be potentially riskier or lead to more challenging missions."

Franz takes a puff on his cigar, reflects for a moment, and then releases the smoke. Finally, he continues.

"We are going to need to get Hermann Krämer's hard drive. That means it will not necessarily be executed at a completely familiar place. We do not believe he lives in Kitzingen, and we are currently trying to find out where he keeps his laptop. It could be at his house, work, or alternate location. This will not be a normal snatch and go. It appears that this mission will be one where he will have to die. It may require Katja to become a bit more familiar with the target. Are you two prepared for that?" Franz asks as he takes another puff on his cigar.

Katja and Rick look at each other briefly before Katja finishes her wine and blurts out, "Yep, I am. I am ready for this. I can do this." She then smiles and winks at Rick while she licks the wine that was on her lips.

Rick smiles back affectionately and says, "we are in."

They both turn to Franz, and he takes a puff off his cigar and smiles. Franz looks out across the nearby hillside and the grapes in the vineyard.

"You know we wait until the right moment to pull these grapes for perfection," he says. "We also waited for the right moment to get us two quality people who are equipped emotionally to manage the missions. Now we must do a bit of research and analysis on Krämer, so we can pick the right time for this. For now, why don't you two go and enjoy the wine fest? In a few days, I will be back to you on this. We must be ready."

Rick replies, "sounds good, Franz."

Katja blurts out, "Yep, sounds good, Franz. But I think some more wine is calling me."

Katja drags Rick back to the wine fest. The band is playing ♪ *Ein Prosit* ♪ and has everyone singing along and drinking. Katja wants to join in, but she is out of wine.

She looks at Rick, "I am getting some more wine. Do you want anything, my love?"

"Yes, I'll have a glass, too, if you don't mind," Rick replies.

Katja smiles and nods as she gets up and works to regain her stability. Once she is on flat feet, she walks to the stand to purchase more wine.

Rick reflects on the conversation they had with Franz outside of town and tries to picture scenarios that could take place on this upcoming mission. At first, he thinks about the possibility of another man kissing Katja or even having sex with her. The thought of Katja possibly having sex with someone else, of course, does not settle well with him. Then his mind moves on to even graver scenarios where she even might be killed. All under the idea of a great adventure. He thinks for a moment, *did we bite off more than we can chew?*

Katja comes back, slightly staggering but smiling with two glasses of wine.

She happily explains, "the gentleman selling the wine did not charge me for the second glass because he said I had a wonderful smile. You know he may be on to something there."

She hands Rick his glass of wine, as he gives her a look of concern. "Are we going to be alright?" he asks.

Katja takes a small sip of her wine, leans over to Rick, and puts her index finger over his lips. She looks into his eyes, "my love, we will be fine. You are my everything. It will be just a mission, and that's it."

Katja then kisses Rick passionately, and after a few moments of the kiss, she pulls back away from him.

"Rick, let's have fun, let's give this life all we got. So, why are we not dancing like everyone else?" Katja asks.

After she takes a few more sips, Katja and Rick get up and dance along with many other Germans at the wine fest. Several songs pass, and they both go and sit back at the table.

Rick picks up his wine glass, looks at Katja seriously and in his best Bogart voice says, "here's looking at you, kid," while raising his wine glass.

Katja gives one of her famous smiles, that one where she grins from ear to ear, and you can count every tooth in her mouth. A smile that everyone loves. She lifts her glass, finishes her drink, and looks Rick in the eye. "Take me home and have sex with me like I am one of your missions." She says as she raises her eyebrows at him.

Rick smiles and responds, still in his Bogart's voice, "we'll always have Iphofen."

As they walk through the Röldeseer Tor, Katja stops and turns to Rick. She looks into his deep blue eyes and kisses him under the gate's shadow.

She can taste the hint of the wine from Rick and pulls back, bites half her lower lip, then grabs his butt. "I think it's time to get home, my love."

Rick smiles proudly as they walk out of Iphofen.

A SIMPLE DAY TRIP

*I*t is Saturday morning, and Rick is up early. He is dressed in his pajamas and walks downstairs to the dining room to find Sabine sitting at the table, drinking coffee, and gazing out the window.

"Good morning, Rick. It is a beautiful day today," Sabine says as she turns to look at Rick.

"Morning, Sabine, it sure looks like it is," Rick replies.

Sabine is already dressed and energized. "Would you like some coffee?" she asks Rick.

"No, no, thank you. I am not a coffee guy," Rick replies.

"That's right, and you told me that," Sabine states. "Why don't we go outside and enjoy the morning sun if that is okay with you, Rick?"

"Sure thing Sabine, sounds good to me," Rick replies.

Two large glass doors led out to the front patio in the living room. The two walk through the doors and sit down on the patio furniture. The birds are chirping in the background as they enjoy the peaceful morning.

Sabine takes a sip of her coffee and then looks towards Rick. "That Emma, she is an interesting one."

Rick, with curiosity, asks, "In what way?"

Sabine smiles at the thought of the young girl's antics.

"She likes to go to the candy store and take a few extra things. So, I talked to the owner there, and I just gave him some extra euros ahead of time. The owner laughed about it. So now, when Emma arrives at the candy store, the owner announces her to everyone," Sabine says. "He goes in a loud voice, 'Emma, it is so good to see you today.'" Sabine smiles. "The owner told me he doesn't do that with everyone, just her. So, they keep a watchful eye out on her."

"I am glad the owner is understanding," Rick replies. "Do I need to give you some euros for that?"

"No, no, no," Sabine replies as she waves Rick off. "You know the same people that pay you, pay me. We are all taken care of."

There is a brief pause in the conversation before Sabine continues.

"Emma is picking up German pretty well, but she is also good at rib kicks with her knees." Sabine says.

"Wow, that went from learning a language to kicking someone's butt quick," Rick laughs. Then, in a serious tone, Rick asked, "so, she is good at martial arts and self-defense?"

"Oh yeah, she can handle her own without a doubt," Sabine says. "I would hate to see the boy that tries to do her wrong. It will not be pretty for him."

Rick laughs at the thought. Emma may be a handful in a few years.

"Now, the three older boys like to get in their mischief quite a bit. Of course, they are boys; what would we expect. But it is not bad mischief; it is just growing up mischief," Sabine explains.

Rick listens attentively and nods in agreement.

"They like to hang out with the kid around the corner. He is a good kid but a few years older than them. It's been suitable for their German language skills. The boy's father owns a construction business. They have all sorts of construction equipment in their backyard along the river. Well, do you know those giant cranes for a skyscraper? I think they are called tower cranes; do you know this?" Sabine asks.

"Yeah, they are huge," Rick replies.

"Well, you know kids and their shenanigans, the neighbor kid got the three boys in that bucket and lifted them up about 15 stories in the air in his backyard," Sabine explains.

Rick was taken completely off-guard, his mouth wide open. "What the hell?"

"It seems the boys have yours and Katja's sense of adventure and living life on the edge," Sabine replies. "Don't be mad at them, Rick, they are just boys."

Rick breathes out and smiles, nodding in agreement.

"Now, that Sebastian is a smart one, that is a fact. He is quiet, but very intelligent," Sabine explains. "He is good at martial arts as well. He likes to kick at the knees and, of course, in the balls." Rick chuckles, but Sabine becomes very serious. "He does this right now because he is small in stature, but later, he will be a force to reckon with regarding self-defense. He is gifted with common sense and book smarts, a rare combination from what I have seen," she explains.

"I agree," Rick says. Being the youngest of all the kids, it is no surprise to Rick that Sabastian has figured out right from wrong by watching his older siblings. Sebastian has had the opportunity of watching his siblings' mistakes and their successes. He is very good at learning and adapting.

After hearing all about his children, Rick looks at Sabine with a concerned look and asks, "so, what about you?"

Sabine gives him a confused look. "Me?" she asks.

"You have been here every day, 24/7, for the last few months and have not left one minute to yourself. So, what about you?" Rick says.

Sabine replies candidly. "Oh, I am good, Rick. Every couple of months, I will leave for one evening but only one. I will let you two know, and of course, Franz will also know, way in advance. What do you Americans say? I will need a booty call," explains Sabine.

Rick busts out laughing, and Sabine replies with a smile, "it is what it is. I get what I need. I get it out of my system, and I am back to you guys."

Sabine puts her hand on her heart and leans back in the chair.

"Sabine, if you ever need more time, don't be afraid to speak up. We are truly grateful to have you in the family," Rick explains.

"Oh, I will. Speaking of a booty call, talk about those boys," Sabine says. "They are curious and are into the girls. I think you and Katja need to be aware of that. You may want to just talk with them on that from a father's perspective," explains Sabine.

Rick nods his head in acknowledgment. "Thanks for guiding me on that, Sabine. As they figure their way through puberty, I probably need to set some ground rules down with the young men," he says.

"So, what are our plans for today?" Sabine asks.

"Oh, I think it is time to get everyone out of the house. I figure we could all drive down to Rothenburg ob der Tauber if that is okay with everyone." Rick explains.

"That sounds great, and I heard it is beautiful there," Sabine replies.

After this, Katja comes walking through the glass door from the living room to the patio still wearing the long shirt she usually sleeps in.

Sabine turns to face her and asks if she would like a cup of coffee.

"Yes, please," Katja replies.

Sabine gets up and goes to the kitchen to find a coffee cup for Katja.

Rick looks at Katja and says, "well good morning, my love."

"Morning my love," Katja replies with a smile as she sits down with her husband.

Sabine returns with a nice warm cup and the coffee pot as well.

Katja smiles. "Thank you, Sabine."

"You are welcome," Sabine replies.

After returning the coffee pot to the kitchen, Sabine retakes her seat on the patio.

"So, how was your evening, you two," she asks with a smile.

"Oh, it was a wonderful time at the Iphofen wine fest. Rick and I had a blast," Katja replied. "Or should I say, the jogger, hm hm and I," Katja laughs.

"Haha, so funny ha ha ha," Rick says sarcastically.

"Oh, I love you, dear," Katja says reassuringly. Sabine gives an awkward smile like she is kind of out of place.

"So, my love, we will go to Rothenburg today and get everyone out of the house. It is about an hour away. It will be fun for everyone. Are you game?" Rick asks.

"Uh, yeah! Let's do it!" Katja exclaims.

"Oh, let's get everyone some breakfast, and let's get going," Rick replies.

After breakfast, and with Sabine in tow, the whole Taylor clan arrives at the western gate of the old town. A large, old wall surrounds the town of Rothenburg. One can walk around the entire city atop the walls, just as they did for centuries in medieval times - walking the walls, overlooking the river and valley – and the family decide to do just that. They walk along the city's western wall, starting from the southernmost point. The boys, along with Rick, are stepping up ahead while Katja, Sabine, and Emma are bringing up the rear, while Sebastian is running along the tower walls. He must stop and wait for some people to pass in some places, then he takes off running again. As Sebastian is about 30 feet in front of the rest of the boys, Rick decides to have a casual conversation with the rest of his sons, Michael, Jonas, and Noah. The discussion is about small things in life, women.

Sebastian stops his dash along the walls to allow a few local teenagers to go through. One oncoming teenager shoves Sebastian against the wall. Rick takes notice of this and looks on with great curiosity. The teenager is about a good foot taller and weighs at least 100 pounds more than Sebastian. Sebastian gets up, and as the teenager laughs and walks away, Sebastian kicks him in the back of the knee. The kick takes the teen to the floor immediately. Then Sebastian jumps on his chest and draws his arm back to strike a facial blow.

"Sebastian! Stop!" Rick screamed.

Sebastian gets up, looks at the boy and says to him in perfect German, "Is it funny now?" and starts jogging along the walls again.

The boys all started laughing. Rick gave a small chuckle himself when he realized his son speaks pretty good German and could defend himself now. Part of him felt really proud; part of him felt sad that his son was also growing up, and he wasn't all small, young, and innocent anymore.

After running by a few lookout towers, Sebastian gets to the defense tower, and Rick calls out, "wait for us; we will get out of the walls here."

Sebastian waits. He keeps looking out the window to the countryside. The men arrive, and the boys all give Sebastian a high five for dealing with the teenager.

Noah starts out laughing, "I guess there is no pushing Sebastian around."

Sebastian is beaming with pride. He is smiling from ear to ear.

Michael chimes in jokingly, "hey Karate Kid, I guess you waxed his butt."

Sebastian's chest swells more and more as each brother complements him.

Jonas laughs and says, "oh a little Jackie Chan," and then gives a karate stance.

Sebastian is eating up all the attention. After all the congratulations, Sebastian looks at Rick as if he wasn't sure if he did the right thing or not.

"Son, never feel guilty for defending yourself," Rick exclaimed. Sebastian smiles. "I think we will find some ice cream later in this town," Rick says. All the boys smile, then Rick puts his arm around Sebastian and says, "I'm proud of you, son." Sebastian is walking a little higher right now.

The ladies arrive; Katja asks, "what's all the high fiving about down here?"

"Sebastian is being a man," Rick proudly responds. "So, let's step out of the city walls here. There is a cool place down the street for a photo. Not far from that, there is a medieval torture museum and after that, I figure we could get some ice cream."

"Cool," Katja approves.

The Taylors make their way to the famous picturesque place in the town known as the Plönlein. It is where two streets merge and form a V. At the center of the V is an old traditional wood-framed house. You can see one tower in the background on one street, and on another street, you can see a different tower in the background. Many paintings and photos have been drawn or taken at the place. The Taylors all lineup, and Sabine takes a few pictures of them at this famous place. They trade out and get Sabine in a photo with the kids and then one with Sabine, Katja and Rick. Then they all walk the cobblestone road towards the center of town. As they walk, almost every house has flowers on every windowsill. It's just part of the German culture. The smell of freshly roasted nuts catches everyone's attention as they see vendors along the street. Then they pass a candy shop on the right-hand side. The kids look in with all sorts of curiosity. Then they approach an intersection. They make a left and come to the Medieval Crime Museum. Outside the Museum, there are two Pillory, where all the kids took their turns standing in them for a photo shoot. Even Rick and Katja got in on it. Sabine took a photo with Emma in the Pillory.

The kids enjoyed the Museum. There were long discussions about some of the torture devices inside the museum. Afterwards, the Taylors walk down the cobblestone street to the local ice cream shop. Along the way, the smell of fresh bread is on one street, the scent of traditional German meals such as schnitzel is on the next street, and the smell of a Turkish Donor is on the next. There is so much to choose from, but today is a day for ice cream.

As the Ice cream melts down the side of their cones and onto their hands as they make their way back to the main market area where they hear music playing. The cobblestone streets of an old city, the music in the background, and the fragrances carelessly drifting in the air are enchanting for the Taylors. In the market an orchestra is playing for everyone. The Taylors make their way past the city hall, sit on the steps, and enjoy the atmosphere.

Katja looks at Sabine, "it's good to get out of the house for a bit, is it not?"

Sabine smiles and agrees.

Rick notices the older boys looking at some of the younger ladies in the band and can hear them talk about which ones are hot and which ones are not. Rick smiles but shakes his head back and forth sideways.

Sebastian tells Rick, "Dad, I liked the torture museum, it was cool, but they had some weird things there."

Rick chuckles. "Yes, they did son."

Emma licks her ice cream and tells Sabine, "Yummy."

Sabine agrees by nodding.

Katja looks at Rick, puts her hand in front of her mouth to kiss her fingertips, lifts her hand and says, "Prima, my love."

Rick smiles with satisfaction.

PEOPLE AT WORK

The next week, Rick returns to work at Harvey Barracks. He is a Sergeant First Class in the Army. He is in good physical shape and works with Lieutenant Sam Moore from Kentucky. They have a good close relationship. Lieutenant Moore is married and has just started his young family. He has two small boys, a newborn and a two-year-old. Lieutenant Moore is a practical officer, a former enlisted man who went to Reserve Officer Training Course, ROTC, in Kentucky and got his bachelor's in History. He is around 5 foot 9, stocky built Lieutenant, with brown eyes, brown hair, and a medium complexion. Lieutenant Moore likes to push for excellence and get the most from people. In fact, he pushes the rest of the lieutenants in the company. Lieutenant Moore enjoys his work and doesn't mind throwing a joke in from time to time.

The First Sergeant in the Company is Ron Garrett. He is all worn out and has no real motivation left. First Sergeant Garrett is simply waiting to retire. He brings no real value to the company. First Sergeant Garrett is from California and has been dealing with a back injury for the past three years. He often does not show up to his own formations and is rarely seen with the Commander. When the First Sergeant is around, he is often slumping over.

The Company Commander is Captain Michael Baker. He is from the East Coast. Captain Baker means well but is held back by not having a quality First Sergeant. Captain Baker is a good man and wants to see the company click on all cylinders. He is an ROTC graduate from Maryland.

Captain Bakers' degree was in Finance. Captain Baker is married, but his family stayed in the states. Many have questioned if the marriage is real or not since no one has seen his wife. Captain Baker is in good shape; he is about the same height as Lieutenant Moore, just a little more weight in the shoulders than Lieutenant Moore. Captain Baker has red hair and blue eyes, and many young female soldiers talk about how handsome he is when people are not around.

The sister platoon has a new Lieutenant that comes from a wealthy family. It seems that he has not faced much adversity in life. Lieutenant John Sawyer is his name, and he takes a passion for not being serious about anything. No one has a good relationship with Lieutenant Sawyer and mainly people just tolerate him. His Platoon Sergeant is inexperienced and doesn't do Lieutenant Sawyer many favors. Sergeant First Class Adam Mosby is a new Sergeant First Class and has spent a lot of time with staff and not the troops. It hampers him when dealing with Soldiers. Lieutenant Sawyer has a problem relating to anyone. Sergeant First Class Mosby is more worried about his fitness; he is 5 foot 5 and has not an ounce of fat on him. He is in incredible shape. Sergeant First Class Mosby is black and single, and he is from Georgia. He is pretty fond of the Bulldogs from Georgia.

Katja is a Staff Sergeant in the same organization as Rick. She runs a section and works in a Platoon. Katja has a female Platoon Leader who is a West Pointer. The Platoon Leader is named Lieutenant Casey Travis. She is extremely smart but also like many West Pointers, thinks she knows it all and no one else does. She is single and enjoys being stationed in Germany. Lieutenant Travis is around 5 foot 9. She is tall and slender. She loves working out. Her skin is pale, and the sun is not her friend. Lieutenant Travis's hair is a sandy blonde to brown at times, her eyes are blue, and she has a good bit of freckles. Her Platoon Sergeant is Sergeant First Class Trevor Jones, an old southerner with a ton of experience. Katja has a good relationship with Sergeant First Class Jones and a decent one with Lieutenant Travis. Sergeant First Class Jones is around 5 foot 10 inches tall; and he is within the weight limits for the Army, but he looks thick. Sergeant First Class Jones is from Alabama, and he has three kids and a wife that lives in the government housing at the neighboring post.

The unit is preparing to conduct a major field training exercise in a few weeks. It will run for about 30 days. They will run split base operations. Part of the unit will be in Grafenwöhr (a German city and also an army training center), part of it will be in Klosterforst, (which is outside of Harvey Barracks) and the rest will be in the rear to run day-to-day operations. As it stands today, Rick will have troops in all three places, and Katja will have troops in Grafenwöhr and the rear. Over the last two months, the unit has prepared for this upcoming field exercise.

Captain Baker has pushed to make sure we do our best in our warfighting environment. He has conducted bi-weekly meetings with his officers within the organization to keep them focused on the target.

KRÄMER MISSION
PARTICULARS

*I*t is around 4:30 in the evening at work, and Lieutenant Moore is chatting with Rick. Lieutenant Sawyer steps into the room and asks, "what are you two assholes doing?"

Rick just shakes his head, but Lieutenant Moore corrects Lieutenant Sawyer.

"Why don't you come in here a little more respectful next time," he says.

Lieutenant Sawyer laughs.

"Maybe next time I will. I just figured I would come down here and see what work actually looks like." Lieutenant Sawyer is a little disappointed because he didn't get a reaction and then decides to leave.

Lieutenant Moore looks at Rick and shakes his head.

"It's hard to believe he is an officer," Lieutenant Moore says.

Rick responds, "we all have our bad apples, Sir."

Lieutenant Moore nods in agreement and smiles.

Katja walks in and blurts out, "you won't believe what that damn Lieutenant just did!" Lieutenant Moore and Rick wait in anticipation. "He walked into the office and called everyone cocksuckers. He said cock is part of the body, and he doesn't see it as a bad word. In his mind, it's all a matter of interpretation. It can only be a bad word if he interprets it that way." Katja steadily shakes her head in disbelief.

Lieutenant Moore, visibly frustrated, says "Staff Sergeant Taylor, I will have a talk with him and probably talk to the Commander as well regarding this."

Right then, Rick's and Katja's phones vibrated simultaneously. Rick pulled out his phone. It said Franz.

Lieutenant Moore stated, "wow, both of your phones simultaneously, that's crazy."

"It's the Nanny," Rick replied.

"Oh, go take care of whatever you two got to do," Lieutenant Moore said with an understanding nod.

As Rick and Katja leave, Lieutenant Sawyer walks in the door. Lieutenant Sawyer blurts out, "why are they leaving?"

Lieutenant Moore stops him. "Don't worry about it. You and I need to talk."

Rick turns to Lieutenant Moore, "Sir, I'll leave you two be, and I will see you tomorrow." "Sounds good," exclaimed Lieutenant Moore.

As Katja and Rick drove home together, Katja reads the message aloud.

Katja and Rick, we have more information on Hermann Krämer. I'd suggest we meet down by the Main River, where no one is close by. Let's say around 7 p.m. Let's meet on the center of the Old Bridge.

Rick nodded with approval as she read the message. Once Katja finished, they didn't say another word during the ride home. Katja thinks to herself about what the mission could entail. Will it be easy and what will it require from her?

When they arrive home, Sabine meets them at the front door. "I have supper waiting on you two. It's Schnitzel and fries," Sabine explains.

Katja gives Sabine a big hug. "Thank you so much, Sabine."

Sabine gives a big smile. "Oh, no worries," she replies.

"Yes, thank you, Sabine," Rick agrees.

All three sit down together at the table and start eating.

"The kids all ate, and they are all doing kids' things. Is everything alright?" Sabine asks.

"Oh yes, just a dumbass Lieutenant at work today," Katja explains.

"Well, get your game faces on; you link up with Franz here soon, right?" Sabine asks.

Both Rick and Katja nod yes.

"Well, you two go get ready and get going," Sabine directs.

The couple heads upstairs to change out of their uniforms into something a little less conspicuous and say bye to Sabine before they head out the door.

Katja and Rick start walking along the Main River towards the bridge around 6:45 p.m. As they walk, both of their minds wonder what all this mission will entail. Katja worries if this will require her to have sex with this guy.

Rick worries if Katja will have to have sex with the guy or if they might even end up having to kill him. As they get close to the bridge, they look at each other and give the other a reassuring stare.

They walk up the stairs on the bridge and a noticeable figure can be seen on the south side of the bridge halfway down. Smoke is visible as he exhales from his cigar. It is Franz.

"Hallo Katja, Rick. How is your night tonight?" Franz asks.

"Not bad," Rick replies.

"Katja and you?" Franz asks.

The aroma from the cigar gently floats past Rick and Katja.

"Oh, I am good just anticipating what the mission will be," Katja says.

"Well, let's get to the mission then," Franz says. "Hermann Krämer is 50 years old, which we already knew. He lives in an apartment in

Würzburg, close to the train tracks. We believe Hermann to be part of the Sharp Sickle. He is about 5 foot 8 inches tall and a little stocky. Strangely he prefers a club that has a lot of GIs at it. The Airport Club is east of Würzburg. He prefers to pick up younger blondes and take them to his apartment." Franz pauses and then looks at Katja, "can you be blonde?"

Katja assures him, saying, "yep, I can do that."

Franz shakes his head in agreement then turns to Rick.

"Rick, we will need you in his apartment complex. Not in his apartment but inside the complex. Can you do that?"

Rick nods and replies, "yes I can."

"Good," replied Franz. "We will need you close by with the ability to get to her rather easily."

Rick nods to signal his understanding.

Franz takes note of this and continues. "A train runs by those tracks every eight minutes until midnight. In a bad case you can beat the door in with the train running, as long as that is before midnight."

"How will I know who it is?" Katja asks. "From my understanding, the Airport Club is like a rave club and there are many people around."

"It is a rave club, but there shouldn't be too many people in their 50s there," Franz replies. "Hermann has a neck tattoo of a sickle on his right side. He has dyed blond hair and will have black eyebrows with brown eyes. Hermann will try to dress young, but once you find the tattoo, you'll know it's your guy."

Katja nods while Rick asks a question of his own.

"So, what is the objective for this?"

"The hard drive," Franz replies. "We believe it is in his apartment, but we are not 100% sure about that. Katja will need a few minutes to locate it without tipping him off, so you will need to give her some time in the apartment. You cannot barge in immediately. Once the hard drive is located, you won't be able to sneak out with that. You will have to either knock him out or kill him. Once it is out, take it to your car, Rick, and we will pick it up from you at your house. We still have some time to prepare for this. Tonight, is Monday night and we want to do this on Friday evening. Rick, this will give you time to understand the apartment. Katja, this also gives you time to become blonde and see the outside layout of the Airport Club. I know that doesn't help you on the inside, but it is a start."

Both Katja and Rick nod in agreement.

"Both of you keep your phones on you during this so we can track you in case something goes wrong," Franz directs.

"We definitely will," Rick replies.

Katja agrees.

"Ok then, so you have the mission, and I will see you two next time with the hard drive," Franz says.

The group separates, each turning to opposite ends of the bridge.

"Bye, Franz," Katja says before they get too far away.

Rick waves bye to Franz.

Rick and Katja walk back along the Main River towards their house.

"Rick, you got me safe, right?" Katja asks.

"I damn sure do, my love," Rick replies while Katja smiles. "This gives me time to figure out how to get into his apartment, so I will know what tools to bring." Katja shakes her head in agreement.

As they approach the house, Rick pauses and gives Katja a big hug. They hold each other tightly for a few moments before entering the house.

Sabine is in the living room waiting for them.

"Hey guys, how did it go?" Sabine asks.

"Not bad, but I have to be blonde," Katja explains.

"Oh, that is too easy; we can do that," Sabine reassures her.

"We have a few days. It won't be until Friday," Rick explains.

"That's good gives you time for an excellent plan and to work all the bugs out," Sabine says.

"I agree; time is good for us on this," Katja explains.

"How about a glass of wine?" Sabine asks.

Both Rick and Katja almost simultaneously reply, "yes."

"Why don't you two sit down while I get it?" Sabine suggests.

Rick sits down, and Katja says, "I will get into some comfy clothes first, and then I'll be down."

Sabine replies, "no problem." She then brings in three glasses of wine and sits down with Rick. They both start drinking the wine. "Rick, are you going to be good on this?" Sabine asks.

Rick replies, "yeah, I feel better about it now."

"That's good, and you do what you have to do, Rick," Sabine said.

He nods his head in agreement.

Katja returns to the living room in a long sleep shirt. Sabine hands her a glass of wine and leans toward Rick and Katja, "Prost!"

Everyone replies, "Prost!"

THE EXECUTION OF
THE SECOND MISSION

*F*riday night, Katja walks out of the house around 8:30 p.m. to catch a cab to the Airport Club. Katja is wearing a white sleeveless blouse that is very low cut and provides a lot to see. Her tummy is showing. Katja exhibits skin-tight black pants down to her ankles that contour tightly to her figure. Her usual pixie cut is bleach blonde and she has her cellphone is in the front right pocket of her pants.

At the same time, Rick gets in his car and quickly drives to Würzburg. He will get situated in the apartment complex where Hermann lives.

Katja arrives at the Airport Club. They had just opened the doors for the evening. She walks in, and it is definitely a dance club. There are a lot of guys in the club and each one turns his head to see what just walked in. Their eyes follow her as she makes her way to the bar. Katja orders a vodka. There are a lot of eyes on her. The music is starting to beat, and many people are on the dance floor bopping to the music. Katja gets her drink and quickly downs it. She notices a few blond guys, but they seem too young to be Hermann. Still, she goes over to check them out for the tattoo.

As she gets closer, one guy grabs her around the waist and tries to pull her in to dance. She pushes him away and the guy looks disappointed. Finally, she makes her way over to where the three young men with blond hair are at. She covertly checks each one's neck for the sickle tattoo but finds that none of them are her guy. Katja starts making her way through the dance floor, checking everyone's neck for the tattoo.

On the other side of town, Rick arrives at the front entranceway of Hermann's apartment complex. Inside there is a stairwell that leads to three floors. On each floor, there are roughly ten apartments. Hermann lives on the third floor in apartment 33, facing the railroad tracks. The complex has a stairwell at each end of the building and Rick decides to sit at the stairwell on the far end of the complex where he can keep an eye on apartment 33.

While Rick waits at the stairwell, Katja has returned to the bar. An hour has passed and so far, no sign of Hermann. She orders another vodka. The bartender is tall and lanky. He has a white shirt on with a black vest. He is cleaned shaved bald.

Another stranger approaches her while she is ordering. "Would you like to dance?" he asks.

Katja notices he is very handsome, but he is definitely not Hermann.

"No, not right now, maybe later," Katja politely replies.

The stranger moves on.

Katja turns toward the door and sees a small group entering the club; four guys and two women. None of the guys are blond, but Katja is relieved that some more women have showed up to relieve some of the pressure of all the desperate man hanging around.

Katja strolls around the club on the off chance that she missed Hermann entering the club. Each group of guys she approaches is enthusiastic with hopes of possibly hooking up with her, but she quickly moves on to the next group before they can stop her. As she makes her way around the club for what feels like the hundredth time, Katja notices an older man with blond hair entering the club by himself. He is of medium build and not very tall. Katja goes back to the bar to order another drink and to get a better view of the gentleman. He turns his head to the left, and she can see a tattoo of a sickle on his neck. This is her guy.

The bartender delivers the drink. Katja throws ten euros on the bar and slowly drinks her shot.

Hermann approaches the bar and orders, "Schnaps, please."

The bartender replies, "Sure."

Hermann turns to Katja and smiles. She can see the tattoo on his neck very clearly. Hermann has over-dyed blond hair with brown eyes and black brows. *Just like Franz had said,* she thinks to herself.

Katja smiles back and says, "Hi, my name is Katja."

Hermann replies, "My name is Hermann." He receives his Schnaps and drinks it. "I haven't seen you here before," he says.

"Yes, this is my first time to come here," Katja replies, and then subtly bites her lower lip. She looks at Hermann and pretends like she is thinking. "Do you come here a lot?" she asks.

Hermann smiles. "Every Friday and Saturday," he replies.

The bartender comes back around and Katja waves at him. "Another vodka."

Hermann pulls out some money. "Make that a vodka for Katja and another Schnaps for me," he says without taking his eyes off of Katja.

The bartender takes Hermann's money and nods in approval.

Katja notices that Hermann is dressed about 20 years younger than he actually is. He is wearing blue jeans and a white shirt. She smiles, and she realizes he is trying hard to be young.

Hermann smiles and asks, "what is so funny?"

"Oh, I just realized you have a very nice smile. It suits you well. It's very pleasing," Katja replies.

Hermann smiles wider. "Do you want to dance?" he asks.

Katja replies, "how about after our drink?"

"Yes, of course," Hermann says.

The bartender brings the drinks. Hermann hands Katja her drink, takes his own and says, "to dancing."

Katja knocks her glass against his, licks her bottom lip, and says seductively, "to dancing."

Hermann slowly sips his drink while Katja downs hers in one gulp. Katja then winks at Hermann as she slams the shot glass down on the bar. Hermann's eyes widen with amazement. He looks surprised and quickly finishes his Schnaps.

Katja grabs Hermann and takes him to the dance floor where techno music is playing. They both bounce to the rhythm of the music. Katja can feel the drinks starting to affect her a little bit. Katja lifts her arms and runs her fingers through her hair as she bounces to the music. Hermann comes closer to her and Katja's smile grows the closer he gets. They draw closer and closer together as they dance until it is body-on-body dancing with the music's momentum. Hermann pulls her tight while dancing. He leans his face into her neck and smells her fragrance. He grins at the smell.

Katja realizes she is a little tipsy. She also realizes that no one except her husband has done this with her since she married and begins to have mixed feelings about it. Part of her thinks this is so wrong. The other part of her is saying she is about to experience something new to her. She is going down a road filled with anticipation and excitement. Her heart starts pounding with this excitement, and she grabs Hermann's waist and wraps her arms around him. Hermann welcomes her advance. Their bodies grind together with the pulse of the music as if they have intertwined as one. She realizes the shots have taken a toll on her, and she is getting dizzy, but she doesn't want to leave the dance floor just yet. She feels that she needs to dance off some of this alcohol.

Hermann seems to unwind a bit more and is as close as he can be. Even with her arms pulling him firmly she is still reluctant. It is not that she is super attracted to Hermann. He is nice-looking, but it is more about someone different. Katja worries she may not be able to stop once they start getting more intimate. Hermann gets a bit more feely with his hands as they dance more and more. He grabs her butt and pulls her tight, grinding his body on her body. Katja grinds back, feeling parts of his aroused manhood as she does. She grabs his butt to pull the thrusts harder and to feel him more. Hermann then reaches up to her blouse and clutches one of her breasts. She can feel his fingers on her nipple. A shot of excitement fills her body. She is savoring the moment, as Hermann is doing this. Katja arches her back, pushing her hips into his, as she smiles and laughs. She returns upright as Hermann leans into her and kisses her, which she fully embraces, as the kiss has her on fire.

"Would you like to go someplace else?" Katja yells in his ear in order to be heard over the music.

Hermann kisses her passionately, signaling a "yes." He takes her by the hand and walks out of the club.

Hermann and Katja walk out toward Hermann's car. Katja is very tipsy, clinging to Hermann with every step.

Hermann is extremely excited. He politely opens the door to his Volkswagen and helps Katja get in. Katja grabs his shirt to pull him toward her and he eagerly leans into the car, kissing her and seizing her breasts with his hands. Katja tilts her head back in excitement. She reaches her hand to the front of his pants. There she can feel that he is still aroused with excitement. Suddenly, Katja sees a flash of light but is unsure if it is the alcohol, anticipation, or an actual light somewhere. She starts to unzip his pants, and then a moment of reality sets in.

Katja thinks to herself, *I got to get him back to the apartment. If it goes any further, we will never get to the apartment.* She fears she will not be able to stop if it continues here. *The whole mission will be a failure if we stay here.*

She places a hand on Hermann's chest and pushes slightly to stop his advances. "Hermann, I am on fire," she says. "We need to go somewhere." Hermann agrees enthusiastically.

"I don't live far away," Hermann replies with excitement.

He cranks the car, and before he puts it in gear, he rubs his hand over the front of Katja's pants. She grinds to the motion of his hand and lets out a soft moan. He breathes out a heavy, eager breath and then puts the car in drive. Hermann spins out of the parking lot of the Airport Club. As he drives, Hermann keeps trying to rub her. Katja is very tipsy, but she also knows Hermann is completely distracted. Hermann can barely contain his excitement.

Hermann makes it to his apartment complex and puts the car in park. He reaches over and kisses Katja. While kissing her, he runs his hand into her pants. Her heart races as his fingers caresses her vagina. For the first time in years, another man has touched her there. She wants to feel him inside of her so badly, but Katja knows she must get him to the apartment.

Katja grabs his arm and says, "let's wait till we get to your apartment."

Hermann gets out of the car and takes Katja upstairs to the third floor. As they walk up the stairs, Katja looks around to see if she can catch a glimpse of Rick by chance but doesn't see him anywhere.

Hermann anxiously walks Katja to apartment 33. He inserts the key and opens the door. Hermann guides her as they walk in. As the door shuts behind them, Hermann pushes her against the door and kisses her deeply, reaching his hand down her pants again. Katja had not felt this way in a long time. It was new and unique to her. Hermann slides his finger inside her, and Katja gasps for a moment and then moans. She reaches down in his pants and slowly grabs his penis. Hermann lets out a deep breath. Katja is filled with excitement as she realizes that this is the first penis she has touched besides Rick's in a long time. Katja's eyes meet Hermann's eyes, and then she quickly unzips his pants. She realizes that soon Rick will be coming through the door. Katja pulls Hermann's penis out through the open zipper, and slowly tugs on it.

Katja puts her other hand on Hermann's chest.

"We have to stop. I really must go to the bathroom. It will only take a moment," she says.

Hermann is frustrated and tries impatiently to force himself on her instead of letting her go to the bathroom. Katja pushes back, and the two begin to struggle.

Outside, a train moves down the tracks and passes by the apartment complex. Rick sits anxiously in the far stairwell, not sure how long he should wait before going in to get Katja. Franz told him to give her a few minutes to find the hard drive, but his mind is flooding with scenarios and what to do.

If I go too soon, I will mess the mission up. If I go too late, my wife could be in danger, Rick thinks to himself. His mind is racing with the possibilities, and time is crawling for him. Rick slowly walks towards the room.

Inside the apartment, Katja continues to fight against Hermann as he grabs her by the head and throws her into the next room. Her head hits the corner of the bed, and she is dizzy from the impact. He charges into the room, grabs her by the waist and tosses her on to the bed. Katja's mood changes rather quickly. She is a bit disoriented from the alcohol and being thrown around. Hermann grabs her pants and starts to pull them off along with her underwear. She is fighting it and realizes she has lost control of this situation. She can feel her feet come out of the pants and she is now naked from the waist down. Hermann's body weight is fully on top of her. She can feel his penis sliding up her inner thigh.

She reaches down and talks calmly. "Slow down, slow down; we have all night, Hermann," Katja says. She touches his penis, and slowly grabs it. With her grip, she gains control of his penis and Hermann.

"Hermann let's take our time," she says as she looks Hermann in the eyes.

Hermann starts to slow down his aggression as he anticipates having sex. Katja pulls his penis closer to her vagina. She can feel the tip of his manhood touch the outer edges of her. Katja's heart is pounding. The front door swings open and Rick steps into the room. Hermann jumps up, confused, not knowing who this is. Rick pulls out his gun with the suppressor and shoots Hermann in the penis. Hermann falls uncontrollably to the floor, screaming frantically. Blood is spewing from Hermann. Katja gasps from the surprise of what just happened.

Rick then walks up to Hermann as he is still rolling on the floor screaming.

"Look into my eyes," Rick demands. "Lift your head and look into my blue eyes." Hermann lifts his head and does as Rick asks. "This is the last image you will ever see. It is my blue eyes," Rick says stoically.

Rick lifts his Beretta and aims it at his forehead. Hermann's brown eyes look back into Rick's blue eyes. Their eyes make contact, and Rick pulls the trigger without hesitation. The bullet penetrates Hermann's forehead and exits out the back of his skull. His body falls forward to the ground, with his face hitting the ground as his soul leaves his body. The smell of gunpowder starts to fill the room. Rick, showing no emotion, looks at the lifeless body lying before him.

On the other side of the bedroom, Katja frantically searches for her pants. She glances at the smoke that slowly billows out from the suppressor at the end of Rick's Beretta and cannot stop shaking as she finally locates her trousers. Katja falls over herself as she works to pull them over her legs. She regains some stability and starts looking around the room for something. Rick looks over at his frantic wife and then back to the dead body, surveying his kill.

Katja continues to frantically scour the apartment. She is in such a frenzy that she is stumbling over herself.

"Katja. Katja, what are you doing?" Rick says, trying to get her attention.

"I am trying to find the hard drive. We got to go. We just killed a man!" Katja exclaims.

Rick grabs Katja by the shoulders.

"My love, slow down. No one knows we are even here. We got time."

He can feel her body shudder in his hands. Katja looks at Rick and kisses him frantically.

"Oh, my love, I went too far, I really went way too far," her voice shakes as she weeps into her husband's chest.

Rick holds her tight, trying to comfort her and help her settle down.

"Katja, no one went too far," Rick says reassuringly. "We all did what we had to do. He was completely off guard. You did that! Let's settle down and find the hard drive. Okay?"

Katja nods her head up and down and then catches a glimpse of something out of the corner of her eye.

"Wait, there it is, right there," she said, pointing to a desk on the far side of the living room. "That's his computer and monitor."

Rick looks toward the computer and forms a plan in his mind.

"We are leaving the monitor and taking the tower," he decides. "It has the hard drive in it, that's all we need."

A feeling of relief came over Katja as her mood changed for the better.

"Katja, send Franz a note. We need mop up," Rick directs.

"Yes, my love," Katja responds as she begins typing.

Within seconds, Katja receives a response from Franz. "They are on their way," she announces.

"Good," Rick replies, then turns to Katja. "My love, I need you to look out the door and make sure no one is in the hallway. If it is clear, we will go down the far staircase, not the one you two came up. You go first and I will follow with the computer tower. Once you are down to the bottom of the stairs, follow me to the car. You got that?"

"Yes, my love," Katja replies, then pauses and thinks for a second. She turns to Rick and says, "wait, Rick." Rick turns to face her. "Let's get his cellphone as well. I mean, he is already dead, and there may be more on there as well," she decides.

"Great idea, Katja," Rick replies.

Katja digs through Hermann's pockets and finds his cellphone. "Here it is. I got it," she says as she lifts it in the air.

"Good, now let's get out of here," Rick replies.

Katja looks out the door, and no one is there. They move quickly down the stairs and to the car. Rick puts the tower in the back seat, and Katja gets in the vehicle. He looks around to see if anyone notices them, and they get in the car and drive home.

Katja cries most of the way home. "Rick, my love. I love you so much," Katja says as they get close to home.

Rick replies, "Me, you too."

As they pull down their street, they see a familiar figure sitting out on the front patio of the house. There Franz is smoking his usual cigar. They stop the car and get out.

"Hallo, my friends, I presume you have something for me?" Franz asks as they approach the front door.

Rick replied, "yes, we do."

"Let's go down to the basement and talk about it," Franz replied.

They all move down to the basement. The basement has two separate rooms with one being occupied by their son, Michael. The group gathers in the second room, across from Michael's.

"So, how did it go?" Franz asked.

"We got the hard drive," Rick replied. "It is in the back seat of the car. We took the whole tower, and Katja got his cellphone as well."

Franz smiled. "Great job, guys. We will have someone pick them up in a few. Katja, how are you doing?"

"I am okay," Katja replied sheepishly.

Franz looks at her, then at Rick and then back to Katja. "Katja tell me what you thought went wrong here," Franz suggested.

"It got too close, we got too intimate, I lost control of the situation," Katja exclaimed.

Franz thought for a moment. Then he proceeded. "You had a plan, didn't you?"

Katja and Rick both nodded yes.

"Did the plan work?" Franz asked.

Rick replied, "yes, it did," while Katja hesitantly nodded.

"But it was close!" Katja exclaimed. "It was close. He was close to entering me. Luckily Rick came through the door."

"I understand," Franz said. "Those can be difficult moments for married couples in this profession. They are not to be taken lightly, either. You and Rick have to be on the same page for this. No matter how far it gets or what level of intimacy takes place. You two do not let that get between you. Tonight, you were the locator and distractor. At all costs, you had to distract. But you also knew Rick was coming through the door, right?"

Katja lifted her head up, looked at Rick. "Yes, I did," she said.

Franz then explained. "That's why we like couples. No one will protect each other as you two will."

Katja laughed at this. "Yeah, Rick shot him in the dick."

Rick and Franz both laughed.

"That there alone is worth a drink, don't you think?" Franz said.

"Oh, I had a lot of drinks earlier tonight, but yes, I could use a few more tonight," Katja exclaimed.

"Then it's settled. Let's find Sabine and have a few drinks," Franz directed.

They all went upstairs to the living room where Sabine was already waiting with the wine in hand. Katja came up to Sabine and hugged her like she was her long-lost puppy. Franz looked at Sabine and nodded in agreement. They each had a few drinks, and then Franz left with the computer tower drive in his car.

Katja and Rick sat on the couch with Katja snuggled into Rick's chest until they passed out together.

KATJA TELLS RICK
ALL THE DETAILS

*A*s morning arrives, Rick slowly wakes up. He could feel drool on his chest from Katja. She was still there. Katja looks at Rick and says, "I have to tell you, I really do."

"Katja, it is no big deal," Rick says. "We will have to do things that we don't expect."

"Rick, let me explain," Katja says. "My love, I went to the club, and it went way farther than I anticipated."

Katja sits and turns away from her husband. She looks, instead, at the floor between her feet.

"Yes, I had a few drinks, but his touch turned me on," she admitted. "You are the one I love, but I did go way too far."

Rick starts to talk but Katja puts her fingers over his mouth.

"Please don't stop me. Let me finish," she says. "This is hard enough. I got to say it, or I can't live with myself unless I tell you. Right now, I can't even look you in the eye."

Rick lifts her chin to look her in the face. Katja looks down at first, then slowly looks at him. Although she tries, she can't stop the tears from flowing down her face as she says, "Rick, Hermann rubbed my breasts," she blurts out. "He rubbed my nipples in the club. Hermann touched my pussy and stuck a finger in me. His dick even touched my wet pussy lips."

A stunning look comes over Rick then he interjects.

"Katja, we know we will do things in the job that we would never do," he says. "I know you will probably have to have sex with some target before it is over with this job."

Katja interrupts, her voice rises as she starts talking fast.

"Rick, you don't understand. I kissed him back. I grabbed his dick, and it felt good in my hand. I wanted him in me badly. I was so wet for him. I would have done anything if you had not come in the door. If he had entered me, I would have enjoyed it. The idea of a new person touching me and doing things that only a woman dreams about aroused me. I know you hate me. Rick, I am ashamed to say it. I mean, I am beyond embarrassed. Do you understand that I am no good to you? I am so embarrassed to say that, but it is the case. I must be honest with you. How can you respect me when I tell you these things? I am no good for you. Could you possibly ever forgive me?"

Rick pauses and then pushes Katja up from the slumping position she has assumed because of her sobbing.

"Katja, we are in this together," he says. "There are going to be times like this. Hell, they may even happen to me. Who knows? But we said we are on this adventure together. That even means the part of the luring. If you did not distract him the way you did with your woman's persuasion, it could have turned out differently. Why can we not have fun with this as we do it? Does that mean we get to go screwing around on each other? No, it only means that we do whatever it takes on the job, even if it is sex."

Katja tries to turn her head away from Rick, but he brings her back to face him with a reassuring hand.

"The job is the job, and we leave it there," Rick continues. "So, if you have sex on the mission, I am not questioning it. Do I want you to have sex and hate it, all for the mission? No, I am not dumb either. If you have to have sex, then have sex. Get your rocks off, distract the guy, kill him or whatever. I would rather you have fun than be in a nervous tizzy about things. Am I delighted you grabbed another guy's dick? No, I am not jumping for joy for that. Am I happy another guy's dick touched your pussy lips? Hell no. But I am quite sure he was distracted while you were doing that, right?"

Katja smiles and laughs. "I would say so."

Rick wipes away some tears from her cheek.

"Katja, you and I are good. There is nothing to forgive, my love. We will do some crazy stuff that no one ever gets to do, and we will have fun with it. Fair enough?" Rick asks.

"Fair enough," Katja replies.

"So, when some spy girl grabs my dick, don't get mad, or when my fingers are in a spy girl's pussy, I don't want to hear it," Rick says jokingly. "When I am balls deep in a secret agent woman-"

Katja interjects, "okay, okay, I get the picture. I will make sure I kill that bitch."

"Looking back, I'm glad I shot the dude in the dick," Rick says matter-of-factly.

Katja hugs Rick and kisses him all over his face. Then she grabs him and says, "let's go upstairs and have some spy sex."

Rick replies, "That's my girl."

SABINE

R ick and Katja are up on a Sunday morning, enjoying the morning. Rick takes a look at the local paper, *the Main Post*. In the paper, a particular article catches his eye.

The article reads, "Würzburg apartment catches on fire, destroys everything in the apartment. No injuries occurred due to the fire."

Rick looks for the address and realizes that it is Hermann's apartment. He broods to himself for a moment and realizes maybe this is what Franz means by mop up.

"Have you seen the paper yet?" Rick asks Katja.

"No, you know I normally don't read that, Rick," Katja replies, then smiles. "I prefer the tabloids, my love. They are far more entertaining."

"I know, but this has Hermann's apartment in the paper," Rick replies.

Katja walks over and takes the paper from Rick, then sits down to read the article. After reading it, she puts the page down and looks at Rick.

"Wow, is that how a mop up is done?"

"I guess so, Katja," Rick replies.

Sabine walks into the room. "Good morning, Rick, and Katja."

Both Rick and Katja simultaneously reply, "Morning."

"Would you like some coffee?" Katja asks Sabine.

"Of course, I would," Sabine cheerfully replies. "So, how was your night last night?"

"Oh, you saw us last night Sabine," Rick replied.

"Oh yes, I did, I mean, after everyone went to bed," she smiled.

Katja brings over the coffee and hands it to Sabine, then she walks over behind Rick, puts her arm down to his chest in a loving way, and replies to Sabine.

"Our night was awesome, Sabine, wasn't it, Rick?"

Rick looks up to Katja, and the two share a kiss. Sabine gives a big smile.

Katja looks around briefly and asks, "what's on the agenda today?"

"Oh, my love, I think just relaxing," Rick replies. "We have a company run tomorrow, so I just want to chill. I'll probably toss the football with the boys this afternoon, and that is about it."

"Sounds good to me," Katja replies.

"It is a wonderful day for relaxing," Sabine agrees with a smile. "How about I make breakfast?"

"That sounds great, Sabine," Rick responds

"Do you want American breakfast or German breakfast?" Sabine asks.

Katja responds, "whichever is easier for you, Sabine."

"German breakfast it is then. I'll need about ten minutes is all," Sabine says.

"I'll get the kids up then," Katja replies.

After the kids are awake and dressed, they come downstairs to join their parents at the dining table. Rick sits on one end with Katja closest to Rick, and Sebastian and Emma along the right side. To Rick's left is Michael, Jonas, and Noah. Sabine sits on the opposite end from Rick. Sabine brought out plenty of different types of Brötchen, various cheese slices, ham, salami, butter, tomatoes, cucumbers, and assorted juices. Before they start eating, each family member grabs the hands closest to them and bows their head.

"Sebastian, would you like to say the prayer," Rick asks.

Sebastian says, "Thank you, Jesus, for our family and the food, amen."

Katja responds, "good prayer Sebastian."

Sebastian gives a big smile. Rick then says, "well, let's dig in."

The next few seconds look like a complete free for all as far as who gets the best Brötchen, meats, etc. Hands are going everywhere but there is a system for each one at the table, but only the individual understands it.

After breakfast, all the kids help with cleanup. Rick goes upstairs and takes a quick shower while the children are busy. Sabine and Katja walk out the living room door to sit in some reclining chairs on the front patio.

"It is a beautiful day, don't you think, Katja?" Sabine asks.

"I agree, it is gorgeous," Katja replies. "I think we should have some wine in a little while to enjoy the morning. It's a slow day, right?" Katja laughs.

"That's a wonderful idea; let's allow the kids to get going first, does that sound okay," Sabine asks.

"Perfect," says Katja.

Rick, finished with his shower and now dressed, steps off the bottom stairs on the main floor with a football in his hands and yells, "boys go get your friends and let's toss the ball around!"

There is not enough yard to throw the football in, so Rick typically throws the ball with the neighborhood kids in the street. The Taylors live on a corner section of the road off the main beaten path. This remote section of the road allows ample space for everyone to toss the football around.

"Katja and Sabine, I got the boys, and we will toss the ball around. Do you need anything before we start?" Rick asks.

"No, we are fine, my love," Katja responds.

Sabine smiles and says, "go have fun."

After Rick runs off to join the boys in the street, Sabine turns to Katja.

"So how did you meet Rick?" Sabine asks.

"Oh wow, we met at Fort Bliss," Katja says. "I was a single parent, and he was a single parent. My son, Noah, and I just arrived at our new duty station at Fort Bliss from Alaska, which was my first duty station. After a few weeks, I ran into Rick there. At first, I didn't care for him, but he did grow on me." Katja says.

"Initially, I didn't know him. We were in the same platoon but different sections. He stood in the back of formations with all the section Sergeants, and I was in a squad. One day he walked up behind my squad and leaned over to one of my Soldiers who failed the PT test on the run and asked, 'how the hell does an 18-year-old, skinny person like yourself, fail the run?'" Katja recalled with a smile. "I replied in a loud voice for my Soldier, saying, 'well, not everyone has 20 minutes to walk it in.' Meaning he wasn't young but old. You could hear a pin drop in the platoon. I didn't know that was the wrong Sergeant to mess with. People were petrified of him. But he admired someone stepping up to him."

"So, you put him in his place?" Sabine laughs.

"Well, no one ever puts him in his place, but it would be me if anyone would," Katja replied. "The running joke is he begged me to go out with him, and I begged him to marry me."

"Is that true?" Sabine asks.

"Oh yes, it is very true, not a bit of embellishment in that at all," Katja says. "Rick would ask me out, and I would turn him down. Initially, I thought he was married. Then I found out he wasn't. He was persistent. Each week he would ask me again for me to go out with him. I would turn him down, then he threw this pitch at me one day," Katja smiles as she is talking. "'Katja,' he said, 'I got to play a company softball game. Could you come over to my house and watch the kids? I have a washer and dryer that you could use while you're there.'" Katja shakes her head sideways and laughs as she explains. "So, I bit on that. I did not know that he took his kids to the softball games; that was just an excuse, and it worked."

"That is sneaky right there," Sabine chimes in.

Suddenly, a blue moped pulls up next to Rick and the boys. Phillip gets off and joins in the street football.

"Go deep, son," Rick yells at Jonas as he tosses the ball about 40 yards down the street.

As he lets it go, all the neighborhood kids go for the ball, running into each other.

"I didn't see any pass interference on that, nope not at all," Rick says jokingly.

One of the older neighbor kids, Johannes, gets the ball and heaves it toward Rick.

Rick catches the pass and then says, "Ok, Noah, you're the target," laughing as he throws the ball. The same thing happens, all the boys run into each other to maul the receiver, and Michael comes up with the ball.

"One thing I loved about Rick; is he is the real deal" Katja says. "He is a real leader, a real soldier, and a genuine person."

"Sounds like you got a good man," Sabine replies.

"I think so," Katja says. "He wanted to have fun, and I wanted to be married. He was not budging on the marriage thing. I had to beg him, and he finally gave in," Katja says while smiling.

"Here it comes, Dad," Michael says as he hurls the ball to Rick.

Rick catches it and then prepares to throw it again. He is on one end of the street by himself, and seven boys are on the other end waiting for the ball so they can maul the next victim.

"Okay, get ready," Rick says as all the kids wait patiently. "This one is for Karl. Here it comes!" Rick throws the ball down the street to the waiting pack of boys.

All the kids jump up for it, and somehow it goes to the ground, where Sebastian scoops it up. "I got it, I got it," Sebastian exclaims as he runs towards Rick with a trail of boys following him.

Emma steps out of the house and watches the boys for a second, then walks over to join in on the street football.

Katja and Sabine take a moment to enjoy the game taking place in the street, then return to their conversation.

"Rick is quite simple," Katja continues. "He's hard-working. Rick likes simple things, and the man loves to travel. He puts his family first in everything. Rarely does he do something for himself. It is all about the family. He has gone well beyond the normal role as a brother trying to take care of his brother Ben who was paralyzed in a car accident. He will do everything to ensure that he is taken care of, even if it kills him. It is all about the family for Rick. So, I got a good one."

Sabine smiles. "How about that wine now?"

"Sounds perfect," Katja replies.

Sabine brings out a bottle of wine and two glasses. She hands Katja a drink and says, "Prost!"

They click glasses, as Katja returns the toast.

Sabine looks at Katja. "So, has Ben always been paralyzed?"

Katja replies, "Oh no, Ben was vibrant and a sight to see. Rick used to show me pictures of him in his prime. He was so handsome. He was driving one day, and Rick was in the car as the passenger, and a drunk driver hit them. Ben was immediately paralyzed, and Rick didn't get a scratch. He feels guilty about that. Rick would not leave his bedside until Ben woke up, and then they practically had to drag him away. Many don't know; Rick and Ben are twins. Ben is actually a few minutes older."

Sabine is amazed by Katja's story. Katja takes a sip of wine, and Sabine pours herself some more.

"Katja, that is just really sad. Oh my, and for him to feel guilty on top of that. Oh, that poor man," Sabine replies.

"Rick really drank a lot after that to deal with it," Katja shared. "He would never do things like drink and drive, but he would drink himself to sleep a lot. I would find him in bed half-naked, passed out, with a bourbon glass still in his hand. It's crazy he would be asleep but didn't spill the glass. That's Rick."

Sabine then asks Katja, "so, what is your story Katja?"

Katja takes a sip of her wine and replies, "Well, now that's a horse with a different color. I am originally from Germany. I grew up here in the north. I finished school in Germany and came to America as an exchange student. I learned rather quickly that America is not Germany. That is not bad; it is just different. Then I had an opportunity to go to southern California and be a nanny. Who wouldn't want to go to California? So, I went and eventually joined the army and went to Alaska. There I got married and had my firstborn, Noah. That marriage didn't work out. Eventually, I made it to Fort Bliss and met a Texas man, Rick."

Sabine nods.

"So, what about you, Sabine? You could be doing anything; why this?" asks Katja.

Sabine turns a bit serious. "I had a man I loved dearly, but he died."

"Oh, I am so sorry to hear that," Katja exclaims. "Please forgive me for intruding."

"Oh, Katja, it's okay. You didn't know. I told you that you all are my second family. Well, my first family was my husband, and we were in the Agency like you and Rick are. We went on a mission; that is where my husband died. He died on the mission," Sabine explained.

"Sabine, are you okay?" Katja asks.

"Oh yes, I am fine, but I wanted to help families through this adventure and ensure they don't make the same mistakes we made," Sabine explained. "Our mission was to retrieve a floppy disk. I thought I could simply drink the guy to sleep and not have sex with him or kill him, and he would just pass out. All went as planned and I thought he was out. I started searching the place, and my husband was outside the door. I let my husband in and the target was in the other room. The guy woke up and I didn't know it. As I was letting my husband into the room, the target rose and shot my husband once in the chest and then in the head. I barely got out of there. My husband was dead before he hit the floor. If I had slept with the target, he would have been completely out, and my husband would be alive. My husband would be here today if I had simply killed the target. We made naïve mistakes, and I never want to see anyone else make the same ones," Sabine explained.

Katja moved over and gave her a big hug. Katja then pushed back a moment and said, "Franz told us you lost a family because of those issues, but it was the wife that died."

Sabine nods her head. "I did die that day. I lost my everything, my poor Hans. Hans was his name, and he was so full of life."

Sabine pauses and looks out at Rick and the boys. "Just like your Rick is full of life. Don't lose that Katja. You got a good thing here; Rick is a good man."

Katja takes that to heart and nods in agreement.

"I would give anything just to sit here and talk with him again," Sabine explains. "I would just listen and soak every second up. Oh, I miss him so much. He used to walk by me and just slap me on the butt for no reason. I thought it was childish, and now I wish he was here to do that just one more time. Hans would sing to the radio. He always messed the words up, but he would butcher those songs with a lot of passion." Sabine smiles, ponders for a second and says, "he would sing those songs at me.

As if they were written just for me and no one else." She shakes her head and smiles in a proud way.

Sabine lets out a deep breath and in a subtle way, changes the mood. "Enough on all that, let's enjoy the day, what do you think?"

"Sounds good, Sabine," Katja replies.

Rick looks out over at the mass of kids awaiting his throw.

"This one's for you Phillip."

He slings the ball down the street. As the ball is still in the air and every kid's eyes are on the ball, out of nowhere, Emma blindside tackles Phillip.

Sabine and Katja look at each other in disbelief.

All the boys look down in shock. Rick comes running up to where Phillip is laying. Emma stands up over Phillip, spits on the ground next to him and says in German, "asshole."

Emma then stoically walks away, like nothing happened.

"Katja, find out what is going on with your daughter," Rick yells to his wife. He then shakes Phillip and says, "son, are you okay?"

Phillip has blood on his chin, he blinks his eyes a few times. He is disoriented. Phillip stammers with his words, still confused. "Yeah, I am okay."

Rick looks at him as he helps him up.

"Alright, let's rub some dirt on that and get you back to playing," Rick says, then turns to the rest of the boys. "Mr. Tough guy here, fellas."

All the kids start laughing.

"Yep, definitely pass interference," Michael exclaims.

Jonas looks at Noah and says, "did you see that tackle?"

"Emma tackled the life out of that boy," Noah replies in disbelief.

"Emma," Katja says in a stern voice. "What was that?"

Emma looks at Sabine.

"He said he likes Julia more than me. So, I gave him something to remember me by," she says. "Lucky that little bitch wasn't out here."

Katja gasps. "Emma, you watch your mouth young lady."

Sabine steps into the conversation. "Emma really liked Phillip. I saw her riding with him on the moped one day."

Katja's demeanor changed a little bit. She is realizing her little daughter is growing up liking boys more and more.

Sabine turns to Emma. "Emma, I know you like Phillip, but you can't beat him up or tackle him."

"I know, I was just mad at him," Emma replies. "He can be so nice, but he knows all the girls like him, so he doesn't like to stick with any one girl. He likes to have more than one girlfriend."

"I know that can be hard but then maybe a boy like that is not right for you," Katja says.

"Mom, I know. But I just wanted him to know I can whoop his butt," Emma says. "I wanted him to know I ended it, not him."

Katja struggles not to laugh, but she chuckles on the inside. Katja looks at Sabine with big eyes. Both are trying not to smile about this.

Sabine turns back to Emma, struggling to keep her face stoic. "Emma, are you okay?" she asks.

"Yes, just mad at him," Emma replies.

Rick makes his way over and asks, "so, what was that about Emma?"

Katja replies, "I think our daughter is growing up more than we realize, my love."

Rick looks at Katja and she just nods her head. He then looks over Emma.

"Emma, are you okay?"

"Yes, dad. I am fine," Emma replies.

"Okay then. Go out there and tackle some more boys, but only after they have the football. Got it?" Rick says.

Emma smiles and scurries off to the group.

BACK TO WORK

*R*ick and Katja arrive at work for the Company run. The First Sergeant asks for a Sergeant First Class to replace him as the lead for the company on the run with the Commander. The First Sergeant is broken and cannot run so Rick volunteers.

"So, Sergeant Taylor, stretch the company out and take them on the run with the Commander. I will be here when y'all return," First Sergeant directs.

Sergeant First Class Taylor salutes the First Sergeant and exclaims, "yes, First Sergeant!"

"Double time, march!" Rick calls out to the company after stretching to begin the run.

He starts calling cadence for the company to keep them in step. The whole unit runs in unison with the song that Rick calls out. They sound like one solid unit.

Rick likes to run backward and face the entire company to project his voice better and see who is not giving their all. The officers are all in the front row behind the Commander and guidon. After Rick calls cadence for about ten minutes, another Sergeant steps out to the side and starts to call cadence. Rick turns forward and goes up to the first row to ensure they keep a steady pace. He notices one of the Lieutenants has a patch on his left arm, showing under his grey PT top. It looks like he possibly had some stitches or maybe a tattoo. It was Lieutenant Sawyer, who is always off the chain, to put it nicely.

Katja is running in the formation with the troops. As she runs, she is bored with it. It is a leisurely pace for her since she is in good shape. As she sings back the cadence along with the rest of the formation, she thinks about things regarding the mission that just happened with Hermann. She feels relieved that they made it through it. Katja tries to think of something that may help her on future missions. *Maybe I should carry a discreet knife or some mace that may stun my target, if need be,* she thinks to herself.

The formation turns as the runners follow the Commander, and Katja starts to get her mind back into the run. The Commander picks up the pace to around an 8-minute mile pace as the run progresses.

Rick yells at a few Sergeants, "watch the stragglers, get them in a formation and bring them home."

The Commander finally slows down and eventually stops. It was a small 4-mile run, just a morning shuffle.

After the run, Rick and Katja return home and take a shower to get prepared for the rest of the workday.

"Rick, did you hear Lieutenant Sawyer bragging about his tattoo?" Katja asked as they are driving back to work.

"Is that what the patch was?" Rick asked.

"I think so," Katja responded.

Rick shakes his head. "Officers normally don't stoop down and get tattoos; they leave those things to the troops. But you know, Lieutenant Sawyer isn't your average officer," Rick says sarcastically. "So, what do you have going on today?" Rick asks Katja.

"Well, the Commander wants to have his weapons and chemical equipment status," Katja replies, to which Rick can't help but laugh.

"What are you laughing about?" Katja asks.

"That means you get to hang out with Lieutenant Sawyer, the chemical officer, today," Rick says still laughing.

"Oh, screw you, Rick, I don't think that is funny." Katja responds irritated.

"Well, that's the life of important people, right?" Rick asks sarcastically.

"Shut up. Just shut up! Ok, so what do you have going on, hmmm?" Katja returns the question.

"Oh, just the usual, making shit happen, that's what I do, all day and every day," Rick exclaims with a smirk.

Katja punches him in the arm and then gets out of the car.

Katja arrives at the Company Headquarters and goes into the conference room where Lieutenant Sawyer is waiting.

"Staff Sergeant Taylor, the Commander has not arrived yet. I got word he will be a few minutes late," Lieutenant Sawyer explained.

"Ok, Sir, I got it. I guess I'll sit here and wait," Katja replies.

Katja looks at her paperwork to ensure everything is in order so she can brief the Commander.

"So, Staff Sergeant Taylor, what did you do this weekend?" Lieutenant Sawyer asked.

Katja thinks for a moment, *what is this guy doing? Is he trying to hit on me? Does he realize who my husband is and what he would do to him?*

"Sir, just hung out at the house with the family," Katja replied.

"So, you didn't do anything crazy this weekend?" Lieutenant Sawyer asked.

This dude is weird, Katja thinks to herself.

"No, Sir. Just some family time," Katja replied.

"Well, I did something crazy," Lieutenant Sawyer responded.

"What did you do crazy, Lieutenant?" Captain Baker asked as he walked into the room.

"Huh, Sir, I hung out with some crazy Lieutenants, that's all, Sir," Lieutenant Sawyer replied to the Commander nervously.

"Well, you will stay a Lieutenant as long as you do crazy shit, ain't that right Staff Sergeant Taylor?" Captain Baker asks Staff Sergeant Taylor.

Katja smiles from ear to ear. "Yes, Sir, it is."

"Do you understand that, Lieutenant Sawyer?" Captain Baker asks in a stern voice.

"Yes, Sir, I understand," Lieutenant Sawyer replied.

After the meeting is over, Staff Sergeant Taylor walks back to her office alone laughing her butt off about what happened. She also found it very weird how Lieutenant Sawyer was acting. Katja started wondering if maybe Lieutenant Sawyer was at the Airport Club or something.

Katja then walked down to Rick's office still smiling from the meeting. As she walked into his office, she saw Lieutenant Moore and Rick discussing something.

They look at her, and Lieutenant Moore asks, "well, how are you Staff Sergeant Taylor?"

"Oh, I am fine Sir," Katja replies.

"I heard you got to spend the morning with our finest officer today?" Lieutenant Moore asked.

"I did, Sir, but it was quite humorous. He wanted to tell me something that he did crazy this weekend, and the Commander came in and told him he will stay a Lieutenant for a long time as long as he does crazy things," Katja explained.

Both Rick and Lieutenant Moore busted out laughing.

"He was acting weird, almost like he was hitting on me or fishing for something. Very peculiar, I would say," Katja said.

"Well, he is strange," explains Lieutenant Moore, "he probably was trying to show you, his tattoo. Hell, he has been bragging about it all day."

"I don't know, but he is weird," Katja says.

"I agree; he is special. He thinks that because he has that Chemical Engineering Degree from MIT, he is smarter than the rest and can just play around all the time," Lieutenant Moore proclaims.

"He has a degree from MIT?" Rick asks.

"Yes, that fool does. Can you believe that?" Lieutenant Moore asks.

Katja and Rick both just shake their heads.

"You want to know what is crazy? I've got to go on a trip with that fool before going to the field exercise. Can you believe that?" Lieutenant Moore explains.

"A trip with him?" Katja asks.

"Yep, his wife, Karen, and my wife, Julie, are friends, and we are going down to the Alps together," Lieutenant Moore explains. "I've got to spend the entire weekend with this fool. Oh, I am not looking forward to that at all." Lieutenant Moore shakes his head side to side.

"That sucks," Rick says.

"Yeah, it does, but Karen and Julie are fellow teachers, and to be honest, Karen is nice," Lieutenant Moore explains. "It's just him that is going to be rough."

"There are many people I'd rather be on a trip than Lieutenant Sawyer; that's a fact," Rick replies.

"Yep, I will be heavily sedated from alcohol on this trip, that's for sure," Lieutenant Moore says.

"So, where are y'all going on this trip?" Katja asks.

"Oh, we are going to the Alps on the German/Austrian border. That little town called Garmisch," Lieutenant Moore says.

"That sounds like fun, don't you think, Rick?" Katja asks.

"Yes, it does, it really does. I heard it is beautiful there, and you can see several countries all from one mountain," Rick recalls.

"Yep, you can; from the Zugspitze. It is Germany's tallest mountain, which you can see Austria, Switzerland, Italy, Germany, and a couple of other countries," Lieutenant Moore explains.

"Sir, you two will be like best buds after this," Rick says jokingly. "You guys will be like the Spearmint twins in the commercial on the ski slopes. Just two peas in a pod."

"Not funny, not funny at all," Lieutenant Moore says defensively.

Katja excuses herself to head home while Rick continues to tease Lieutenant Moore and close out some work. She stops off at the local bakery to pick up some bread on her way. Sabine usually does that, but Katja wanted to help relieve some of Sabine's personal stress and allow her to decompress. This pitstop allowed Rick to arrive home from work first.

Sabine met him at the door and asked, "where's Katja at?"

"Oh, I have no idea; she left before me," Rick replied. "I am sure she will be home soon."

Sabine smiles and says, "Well, I have to tell you something. It seems Michael has a little German girlfriend."

Rick responds in slight disbelief, "really?"

Sabine smiles and says, "She is downstairs with him now."

Rick looks at her a second, smiles a mischievous smile, and walks downstairs to Michael's room. He opens the door without knocking and startles Michael and a young, blonde girl who happen to be kissing each other.

"Hm, hm, someone you want to introduce me to, Michael?" Rick interrupts.

The two teens jump from surprise and quickly separate. Michael turns beet red. "Uh, yeah," he stammers. "Dad, this is Angelika, and Angelika, this is my Dad."

Rick walks in and extends his hand to Angelika who is also red as a beet. "Nice to meet you, Angelika. Would you be joining us for supper?"

Angelika looks at Michael and then back to Rick. "Yes, if that is, okay?"

"Well, I'm the dad, and I make the rules, so I guess it is okay," Rick responds. "Just leave the door open from now on, Michael. Are we straight?"

Michael responds, "yes, dad."

Rick walks back up the stairs and informs Sabine of the dinner guest.

"Sabine, we will have one more for supper tonight," he announces.

Sabine smiles approvingly. As Sabine walks into the kitchen, Katja opens the front door.

"I got some bread from the baker," she states.

"Good," Rick responds. "We have a guest."

"A guest?" Katja repeats.

"Go ask your son, Michael," Rick replies with a smirk.

Katja goes downstairs and yells, "Rick, what is this?"

Rick smiles and says, "well, my love, that is Michael's guest. Did he not introduce her to you?"

Katja gives Rick a shocked look and then goes back upstairs.

THE DATA

Katja and Rick are up early for morning PT. The Commander is allowing anyone that wants to run Schwanberg Hill instead of unit PT they could. So, Katja and Rick decided a change in scenery would be nice and drove up to the base of the hill to meet up with several unit leaders there.

The hill has a nice steep running route to the top that winds back and forth through the forest and vineyards. It is a beautiful place for a run. It is situated east of Kitzingen, and when you get to the top, you can see over the town.

After a few minutes of stretching, everyone is released to run it at their own pace. Rick and Katja decided to take an easy-paced run to the top together. As they start their run, Katja notices who all group together for the run. Of course, the lieutenants were all in one group together. That is what young officers do. Lieutenant Moore, Lieutenant Sawyer, and Lieutenant Travis are all jogging together, chatting as they move up the hill. A few junior Sergeants were in one group, and the senior Sergeants in another. Rick and Katja stick together to enjoy their pace. As they approach the vineyards, they notice soldiers running from other units.

Rick and Katja are the first from their unit to make it to the top. They stop for a few minutes and look around, enjoying the scenery. The sun is up, with its rays touching across the valley. The rows of grapevines headed down the hill, all in nice rows, with this year's grapes just waiting for harvest. The town of Kitzingen is in the distance.

Rick stands up very proud. He looks at Katja and stretches his arms out. In a very authoritative voice, Rick says, "my queen, all that you see below, is mine. For this is my kingdom." Rick drops his proud stance. "I believe that is how the medieval kings would have said it, probably from this exact spot, even."

Katja chuckles. "Rick, our little shanty over across the river, let's see if we can find it. You know the king likes to send a knight and requests my, hmmm." Katja pauses, lifts her eyebrows a few times, then smiles perversely as she continues, "personal service. If you know what I mean." She finishes with a wink at Rick.

The two look out at the view of Kitzingen, trying to locate their house. As they scan the landscape, they hear, "Stopping is for losers," coming from Lieutenant Sawyer as the officers turn around and head back down.

"Well, this loser isn't sweating like some young officers are," Rick blurts out. "I am just saying; maybe you officers need to run a bit more. That's a shame, and I am ten to fifteen years older than you young puppies."

Rick rolls his eyes as the group of lieutenants start down the trail. "Let's head down," he says to Katja.

Katja hits Rick to get his attention.

"Look at his arm," she says excitedly. Rick squints at her, trying to figure out what she is talking about. "Rick, the tattoo on his arm," she says again.

Rick, when he finally realizes what she means, replies, "what a dumb officer," as he shakes his head.

"Okay, let's head down," Katja restates.

They take their time as they make their way down to the bottom of the hill. When they finally arrive, the officers are already gone.

Rick looks around at the empty space.

"I guess no one waits on each other around here, so let's get."

They both get in the car, and Rick starts driving in the direction of home. As they pull away, Katja checks her phone.

"Rick, we got a message from Franz. He wants to meet us tonight."

"Do we know when or where?" Rick asks.

"Yep," Katja answers. "Eight p.m. at the bridge."

"Okay, got it, but we've got work to do today," Rick replied.

"Yes, my love, we have that boring ole Army work to do," Katja says sarcastically.

Throughout the day, Katja's mind is all over the place. She keeps reflecting on the mission with Hermann and all the scenarios that could have turned out different. They range from having sex with him to him killing her and Rick. Katja thought a lot about what Sabine had said about missions and what happened to her husband. All these thoughts and scenarios she didn't like. Katja decides that she should have some alternate means of handling these scenarios. She has made up her mind. She is determined to remain in control of the situation for future missions.

Maybe a small push handle dagger to keep on me, she thinks. A small dagger she can keep in her belt line or pocket, that no one will know about. *It might not be much,* she thinks. *But it very well may be just enough to get the job done and keep me and Rick alive.* To Katja, that is all that mattered.

Rick focused on work throughout the day. At times his mind would drift to the mission with Hermann as well. He thought that Hermann would have probably had sex with Katja if he got there any later.

If she resisted too much, Hermann might have even killed her, he thought to himself.

Rick has no remorse for killing Hermann whatsoever. In fact, after Hermann was on top of Katja and Hermann was about to fuck her, Rick savored killing him. *Perhaps instead of killing Hermann immediately, I should have asked for some information from him first,* Rick pondered. *Maybe let the situation marinate a bit before killing him.*

But even still, overall, it was satisfying to shoot the bastard twice.

After work, Rick and Katja arrived home to find Sabine at the door waiting on them.

"Hey guys, I got supper ready, and I will have the kids down early tonight," she told them. "There is no Angelika here tonight; she may be back tomorrow, though. Who knows?" Sabine smiles.

Everyone goes to the dinner table and has a seat.

"Jonas, would you like to lead in prayer tonight?" Katja asks.

"Sure, Mom," Jonas replied.

Everyone grabs their neighbor's hands, bows their head and Jonas starts the prayer.

"Dear Lord, bless each of our family members, look over each of us, don't forget about Uncle Ben, Lord, and bless this food that Sabine prepared. Oh, one more thing, Lord, don't let Michael get sick from all that kissing he has been doing, amen!"

Jonas proudly smiles.

Michael hits him.

"Not funny, Jonas," Katja says.

"Not in the prayer, son," Rick scolds. "You know better than that."

"Michael, smoochy, smoochy," Sebastian chimes in mockingly.

Michael turns red.

Sabine comes to Michael's defense. "I think it is okay for a, hmmm, young man to kiss a young lady," she responds in a serious tone.

"I agree," Katja replies. "Just not too many kisses."

After dinner, Sabine clears the table then turns to Rick and Katja. "I got the kids; you two have something to do. Go get ready," shooing them away.

Rick and Katja nod their heads in response then go upstairs to get ready.

Afterward, the pair head out the door and begin walking the Main River towards the Old Bridge. They can see a familiar silhouette standing about in the middle of the bridge on the south side as they walk. It is Franz. Stepping closer, the aroma from his cigar fills the air as Franz lets out a puff.

Rick and Katja walk up to him, and Franz greets them.

"Hallo, my friends. It is good to see you guys. I trust things are going well."

"I would say so," Rick responds.

"Yep, I agree with Rick," Katja jumps in. "Things are going well."

"So, we can talk here unless you see someone approaching," Franz says looking over his shoulder. "I ask, Rick and Katja get close to me. Rick, you keep an eye on the west end of the bridge, and Katja, you keep an eye on the east end," Franz directed.

"I got it," Rick replied.

"Yep, I am watching," Katja replied.

"Well, you two did great work," Franz begins. "The hard drive and the phone both provided us with a lot of information. It appears we have a sleeper cell that has awoken, and a good bit of it is around this area here. I told you both about the Red Army Faction, which was busy in the 60s through the 90s. Most of it died, but it seems a few members have revitalized it, and are now known as the Sharp Sickle."

Rick and Katja turn to each other in surprise at this revelation.

"They like to go by that now," Franz continues. "From what we understand, a good portion of them wear the sickle tattoo but not all of them. They have a really big goal. They want to poison a prominent world leader. In their organization, they have a chemist who they call The Mixer. That is all we know about it. Supposedly he will mix a deadly concoction for an unknowing leader that will kill him. From what we understand so far, we know that they have at least nine active members, but we do not know all their names yet. We do know that there are at least three females in the group. One is German, one we believe is from Poland, and we think one is Russian. The German is Lena Klein, the Pole is Gizela Gorski, and the Russian is Sasha Popova. We know three of them are males, and we are unsure of the other three. One of the men is from Russia, and his name is Pasha Stephenov; the other two are of German origins, we believe. Their names are Andreas Lange and Otto Braun."

"Someone is coming," Katja quickly interrupts.

"So, Rick, how was your PT run?" Franz changes the subject as the stranger passes by.

"It was okay, Franz," Rick responds, trying to act natural. "Nothing a man from Texas couldn't handle,"

"Yeah, it was an easy run, to be honest," Katja jumps in.

"He's gone now," Rick announces after checking their surroundings again.

Franz gets back to business and turns to Katja, "Katja, are we good on your end?"

"Yes, we are," Katja responds and then remembers something. "Oh, before we get started back, Franz, I need something."

"What do you need?" Franz asks.

"I need a push handle dagger," Katja replies. "Not a big one, just about two to two and a half inches. You know, just big enough to get the job done."

"Of course," Franz nods. "It will be at your house tomorrow before noon. Is there anything else?"

"Nope, that is it," Katja cheerfully replies. Franz continues.

"Okay, so we have six of their identities, and we have some background on them," Franz summarizes. "We will gather more intelligence on them over the next few days and hopefully find out who the other 3 are, especially the mixer. Once that is done, this mission may be very different. We may have you conduct more surveillance on them, so we can find out who the mixer is. Hopefully, we can find out who the target is and the expected time for this to occur. Understand you have not dealt with characters this shady yet, so you will need to be always on your toes."

"We understand," replied Katja.

Rick nods his head in agreement.

Katja then asks, "will we need to go by our real names in this or resort to those names on the passports you have for us in the safe?"

Franz thinks for a moment and then replies, "keep those in the safe for now. Do memorize those aliases in the passport, but I don't see a need to use them for this mission."

"I already have them memorized," Rick replies.

"I would expect nothing less," Franz chuckles. "How about we meet in a few days? I should have a mission for you by that time."

"Sounds good," Rick responds.

"Well then," Franz says. "You two have a lovely evening."

"Bye Franz," Katja blurts out and waves.

Franz heads off the bridge on the east side while Katja and Rick head toward the west side.

The couple strolls down along the Main River and then make their way home. As they reach the front door, they pause.

Katja looks at Rick and gives him a long passionate kiss.

"I love you, Rick," she says when they finally break apart.

Rick responds, "Me you too, my love, me you too."

TRAINING MEETING

*R*ick and Katja get up early the next morning and head to work. As they drive, they discuss what Franz had told them the night before.

"Rick, that is a lot of people in the Sharp Sickle," Katja says.

"It is, my love," Rick answers, agreeing. "I didn't expect that we would focus on this many people at one time."

"Me either," Katja replies exasperated.

A moment of silence takes over until Rick brings up Katja's request from the night before.

"So, you need a dagger, do you?" He prods.

"Chut up!" Katja says with a quick slangish tone. "Yes, I do," she smiles.

Rick's smile grows more considerable, and he chuckles. "Well, if you are out there seducing all these men, I guess you need some protection."

Katja hits Rick on the shoulder. "Shut up, you fucker," says as she shakes her head.

Rick, satisfied with the reaction he got from his wife, changes the subject.

"So, what do you have going on today?"

"Oh, just work, my love. Just work," Katja responds.

Rick laughs again and looks at her.

"Okay, that's enough," Katja yells.

Rick finally backs down from giving her a hard time.

"Oh," Katja blurts out. "We have a training meeting later in the day. I guess I'll see you there."

"Yep," Rick nods. "I got some work to do with Lieutenant Moore, and then it's the boring training meeting."

When they arrive, Katja heads to her office and finds Lieutenant Travis is there waiting for her.

"Staff Sergeant Taylor, how are you today?" Lieutenant Travis asks.

"Ma'am, I am good. What can I help you with?"

Lieutenant Travis is a West Pointer, and she is a very proud officer. Rarely does she talk with the enlisted Soldiers unless it involves work.

"Can we go to your office?" Lieutenant Travis asks.

"Sure, Ma'am," Katja responds.

The two enter the office and each take a seat in the middle of the room.

Lieutenant Travis looks at Katja and says, "I got two things I would like your help with, if that is okay."

Katja responds, "sure, whatever it is."

"Staff Sergeant Taylor, we have a training meeting soon, and I would like to get the status of my platoon's weapons and the company's weapons," Lieutenant Travis says.

"That's too easy, Ma'am," Katja replies. "Let me get you a copy of our printout, and I'll go over it with you."

Lieutenant Travis smiles and says, "awesome."

Katja then asks, "what's the second thing?"

Lieutenant Travis sheepishly looks over her shoulder. "I ask that this stays between us if that is, okay?"

"Certainly, Ma'am," Katja replies.

"Well," Lieutenant Travis begins. "You know I graduated from West Point."

Katja nods.

Lieutenant Travis continues, "I didn't really date any guys there, but there is a guy in the sister Battalion that I like. Could you help me do my hair?" she asks. "I love your haircut, but I really loved it when you changed it to blonde. Could you help me with that?"

Katja smiles and asks, "Is he cute?"

Lieutenant Travis smiles, "yes, he is. He is handsome and outgoing."

"Ma'am, I'd love to," Katja happily responds. "So, when do you meet him again? When do you want your hair done by?"

"Well," Lieutenant Travis says nervously. "I would like to do it before the weekend if that is okay?"

"Then how about tonight?" Katja responds.

Lieutenant Travis's eyes light up, and she grins from ear to ear. "Yes, yes. Oh, I need to get this length cut. I want the pixie cut as you have," she says excitedly.

"We can do that," Katja says. "I just need the color you want."

"I'll bring you a picture of it before lunch. Is that good?" Lieutenant Travis says.

Katja replies "Yes, Ma'am it is. I know someone who can help; you just follow me home after work today, is that alright?"

Lieutenant Travis smiles. "Yes, it is Staff Sergeant Taylor."

After Lieutenant Travis leaves, Katja calls up Sabine.

"Good morning, Sabine."

Sabine, cheerful as always, responds, "good morning, Katja."

"I need a favor, if that is alright?" Katja asks.

"Of course, anything," Sabine responds.

Katja explains the deal with the Lieutenant and all. "I'll be by real quick around lunchtime to drop off the photo for the hair color. Could you pick it up for me? I will probably need your help to do this make-over with her if that is okay?"

"Oh, it certainly is," Sabine replies. "Also, Franz dropped off a small box for you; he said you would know what it is."

"Awesome, I sure do," Katja happily replies. "See you in a few hours."

At lunch, Lieutenant Travis brings a photo from a magazine of the color she wants to Katja.

Katja looks at it over as Lieutenant Travis stands by, anxious and nervous.

"Oh, we can do this," Katja confirms. "So, after work, just follow me home."

"Sounds good, Staff Sergeant Taylor. See you then," Lieutenant Travis replies.

Katja heads home quickly during her lunch break to bring the picture to Sabine.

When she arrives home, Sabine meets and greets her with a smile.

"Hallo Katja, I got your box for you."

Katja is very excited and quickly opens the box up. She pulls out a push handle dagger in a concealed sheath with a clip that will allow it to attach to something.

"Yes, yes, yes!" Katja says enthusiastically.

Sabine laughs at Katja as she dances around the kitchen.

Suddenly Katja stops.

"Oh, I got something for you," she says handing Sabine the picture. "Here is the photo for the color that we need."

Sabine looks at it and smiles. "This will be easy," she says. "There is a little store across the river that has hair color. I'll get it in a few."

"Sounds good," Katja says. "The Lieutenant will follow me home after work today."

"This is no problem," Sabine replies, then smiles. "In fact, would we like to have some wine tonight as we are doing this?"

Katja smiles approvingly.

"Perfect." She pauses, then says, "Thanks, Sabine; I got to get back. We have a meeting shortly."

"Cheers," Sabine replies.

As Katja heads back to the base, she feels pretty good about getting the dagger. Her mind goes over scenarios with Hermann where she could have used the dagger to change the outcome. Even though the mission was a success, she feels they could have executed it better, or the slightest change would have altered events tremendously.

Rick walks towards the company headquarters with Lieutenant Moore. As they approach the front door, Rick sees Katja pulling up. He proceeds into the building with his Lieutenant and has a seat in their usual place in the room. Katja then walks in and takes a seat towards the end of the table close to Lieutenant Travis. Everyone in the room is waiting for the Commander to arrive.

When the Commander finally walks in, the First Sergeant shouts, "Company Commander."

Everyone immediately stands at attention.

"Carry on everyone," Captain Baker replies. "Please, take your seat. I want to introduce a new officer to the organization, Lieutenant Melanie Young. She is a graduate of the University of Michigan ROTC program. Melanie has a degree in pharmaceutical sciences, and her father is a pharmacist as well. Now she is a logistician, so I expect each of you to welcome her in and make her part of the company."

Lieutenant Young stands at about 5 foot 7 and weighs about 130 pounds. Her hair is brown; her eyes are green with olive skin and a curvy figure.

"So, let's get on with the meeting. I want to make sure we have our best foot forward for the upcoming field exercise in roughly a month. I want the soldiers to experience the full gambit of everything it takes to be a soldier in combat," Captain Baker explains.

After the meeting, as everyone is leaving, a couple of the other lieutenants gather Lieutenant Young up to ensure that she has some friends. Rick and Katja head back to their work areas.

As they walk together, Katja looks over to Rick and says, "hey, I got someone coming over tonight for a bit."

"Who, my love?" Rick responds.

Katja smiles and says, "Lieutenant Travis. I will tell you about it later."

Rick looks at her surprised. "Okay, see you at home."

After work, Katja waits in the parking lot next to her car to see if Lieutenant Travis will arrive or not. While she is waiting, she notices several soldiers eyeballing Lieutenant Young as she walks with Lieutenant Sawyer.

"Hey Staff Sergeant Taylor," Lieutenant Travis happily calls out as she walks across the parking lot. "Are you ready?"

"Sure, Ma'am," Katja replies. "Just follow me."

As Katja pulls into the front of the house, Lieutenant Travis follows right behind her. Katja gets out and waves at Lieutenant Travis to follow. They walk up to the door, and Katja opens it.

In the kitchen, she can hear Sabine, "Hallo, Katja, and I'll be right there."

Katja looks at Lieutenant Travis, "come on in; it is okay."

"Oh, my goodness, this is big," Lieutenant Travis replies. "I just have a small apartment."

"Well, you are single, Ma'am," Katja responds. "We have a robust family, trying to save money."

Sabine comes around the corner. "Hallo, my name is Sabine," she says as she reaches her hand out to Lieutenant Travis.

Lieutenant Travis smiles and says, "I am Casey; very nice to meet you."

Katja jumps in to introduce her. "Lieutenant Travis, Sabine is our nanny, but she is really our everything."

Sabine smiles and drops a knee to take a bow. Sabine then asks, "is wine, okay?"

Katja responds, "yes, of course." Lieutenant Travis is hesitant, and Katja says, "she just said yes also." Everyone smiles as Sabine goes back into the kitchen to get the wine.

"Let me give you the house tour while Sabine gets the wine," Katja says.

Lieutenant Travis nods in agreement.

After the tour, Lieutenant Travis and Katja make it back to the living room and sit down as Sabine comes out with the wine, and she passes a glass to everyone.

Sabine lifts her glass to the others and says, "Prost!"

Katja clicks her glass with the other drinks and responds, "Prost!"

Lieutenant Travis is very hesitant, so Katja leans over to her and says, "always say Prost when you initially get a drink with others."

Lieutenant Travis smiles and says, "Prost!"

Lieutenant Travis then looks at Katja.

"Wow, I don't know how you do it?" she says. "You have five kids, a handsome husband, and you are in the army. You got it all together, and I have trouble keeping me together."

"Years of practice and lots of help," Katja laughs. "A lot is, never put anything off and make sure I fully prepare for the next day. And, since we got to Germany, a lot of help from this great lady, Sabine," Katja explains.

Sabine smiles as she takes another sip.

"So, before we get started, tell us about this man you like," Katja says.

Lieutenant Travis's eyes light up.

"Oh my, he is in the Air Defense Battalion. He is probably 180 pounds and about 5 foot 9 or 10. He is very well built, he has brown hair, brown eyes, and tan skin. He is an officer, too, not a West Pointer but an officer. His name is Lieutenant Piper, and he is a Platoon Leader in his unit. He is physically fit, and we went out once."

Sabine takes another sip. "And?" she says. "How did that go, Casey?"

Katja and Lieutenant Travis laugh.

"Well, we went out to eat in Würzburg, we had wine, we walked by the Fortress," Lieutenant Travis says. "Oh, my, it is gorgeous down there. We even went back to his place." Lieutenant Travis stops there.

Sabine and Katja leaned in attentively waiting, and Katja finally blurts out, "okay, then what?"

"Well," Lieutenant Travis says hesitantly. "We kissed and stuff, but I stopped it and told him that, I don't go do certain things on the first date. He looked at me and said, it's okay. It just gives me someone to get attached to. He is a great guy." Lieutenant Travis finished with a big grin.

"Way to go, girl," exclaimed Katja. Sabine then said, "well, let's get your hair done so next time you tell him no, he will beg you."

Lieutenant Travis gave a big smile.

"Okay ladies," Katja says as she stands up from the couch. "Let's go upstairs and get this done."

Lieutenant Travis then asks, "can we bring the wine?"

"Of course," Sabine laughs.

When Rick arrives home later in the day, he walks in, and says, "Hello, is anyone home?"

He hears giggling and muffled words from upstairs.

"My love, we will be down in a few," Katja calls out followed by a lot of laughing.

Rick decides to go downstairs to check on Michael. As he gets to Michael's door, he notices it is shut. Rick thinks that Michael has his girlfriend in there again, so he knocks once and then enters. Michael is lying in bed listening to music on his earphones. He doesn't even notice Rick, so he leaves and shuts the door behind him. He goes up to the main floor and then to the second floor, where all the commotion is. He finds Emma playing with Sebastian in her room.

Sebastian runs to Rick and hugs him.

"Hey Dad, I love you. How was your day?" Sebastian asks.

Emma stays on the floor and looks on. Rick goes into the room with both of them and sits on the floor.

"My day was good," Rick replies. "What about your day and Emma's day?"

"My day was good, Dad," Sebastian replies.

"It was good," Emma says. "Just the same ole routine, boring schoolwork."

Rick nods in an understanding way. "How long have they been in there?" he asks, pointing behind him, toward the hallway.

Emma responds, "probably an hour."

"So, they probably should be done soon, right?" Rick asks.

He looks at Emma and Sebastian with a questioning look. Both Sebastian and Emma nod in agreement.

The bathroom door finally opens. Sabine and Katja come out first.

"I would like to introduce Ms. Casey Travis, Miss West Point herself," Katja announces.

Lieutenant Travis steps out and smiles.

Rick is shocked. "Wow, Ma'am, you look gorgeous."

Then Noah and Jonas come out to see what is going on.

"Is this the same lady that was here earlier?" Jonas remarks.

"Yep," Sabine says as Jonas hits Noah on the chest and giggles.

"Do I look bad?" Lieutenant Travis then asks the boys.

Jonas shakes his head. "Nope, you look hot," he says with a smirk as they head back into their room.

Lieutenant Travis is on cloud nine.

Katja, satisfied with her work on Lieutenant Travis, gives Rick a hug and a kiss, then gently touches the side of his face. "You ready for supper, my love?"

He smiles approvingly.

Katja looks over at Lieutenant Travis.

"The Lieutenant is joining us as well," she says.

Lieutenant Travis replies, "oh no, I couldn't intrude."

"Ma'am, it's a done deal," Rick steps in. "Let's all help Sabine with the table. Come on, kids, everyone pitch in."

When the table is set, everyone is finally seated. Lieutenant Travis is sitting between Emma and Sebastian.

Rick looks across the table "Noah, would you like to lead us in prayer?"

Noah smiles as everyone grabs each other's hands and bows their heads. Noah says, "Lord, thanks for this great food that we are about to have. Thank you for the good things we have and our good friends, oh and bless Uncle Ben, Amen."

Once the prayer is done, the normal free-for-all begins at the Sawyer house.

"If you don't grab something, you might not get something," Emma tells Lieutenant Travis.

They both smile at each other.

Rick starts with his nightly supper questions.

"Sabine, how was your day today?"

"It was great.," Sabine responds. "I got to work on a beautiful lady's hair."

Then Rick goes to Noah. "How was school today, son?"

"It was good, Dad, just a normal day at school," Noah responds. "Oh, I was selling students sodas from my backpack. The principal called me into his office. I was selling them for a nickel less than the machine was selling them for. He liked my entrepreneurial spirit but said I couldn't do that at school anymore."

Rick laughed. "So much for free enterprise, I guess."

Katja then turns to Emma. "So how was your day at school today?" she asks.

"Mom, she likes Randy at school," Jonas blurted out before his sister could answer.

Emma immediately turns red. Katja first scolds Jonas at the table, then she looks at Emma and says, "Is this so, Emma?"

Emma responds while looking down at her plate. "Yes, Mom."

Katja then asks, "does he like you, Emma?"

Jonas jumps back in, "oh, he does Mom, he sits with her at lunch."

Katja looks at Emma. "Maybe we should talk about this after supper, would that be, okay?"

Emma nods her head in approval. Rick then steps in and says, "Jonas, so how was your day?"

"Oh, Dad, it was great I got to see Emma and Randy share a drink," Jonas replies laughing.

"I think that is enough, son," Rick says sternly.

"Yes, Sir," Jonas quickly responds.

Katja then turns to Michael. "And how was your day, son?"

"It was good, Mom," Michael responds. "Just a lot of homework as usual."

Katja then looks at Sabastian and says, "So Lieutenant Travis, how was your day?"

Sabastian gives a face of you got me.

Lieutenant Travis says, "to be honest, can I call you Katja?"

"Yes, you may, Casey," Katja replies.

Lieutenant Travis smiles. "This has been one of the best days I've had in Germany. I am around family. Lieutenants don't get that too often."

"I am glad to hear that. It's good to have you over," Katja replies. "I guess that is everyone, so let's enjoy this food Sabine made."

Sabastian clears his throat in a demanding way, and Sabine says, "Sebastian, what about your day today?"

"Well," Sabastian starts as he grins proudly. "We got to play football at school, and I caught three passes."

Rick then asks, "what about your schoolwork?"

"Dad, it is so easy," Sabastian replies. "I could go to sleep in class and still pass."

The whole family, as well as Lieutenant Travis, laughed and the conversation at the table did not stop for quite a bit.

BEGINNING INFORMATION ON SHARP SICKLE MEMBERS

K atja and Rick arrive at work after PT the next day. Katja returns to her office where Lieutenant Travis is waiting for her.

Lieutenant Travis looks at Katja, "Staff Sergeant Taylor do you mind if we go inside for a bit?" she asks.

Katja responds, "no, not at all."

They walk into her office and shut the door. Lieutenant Travis looks around the room to ensure no one is there and then gives Katja a big hug.

"I just wanted to say thank you so much to you, Sabine, and your whole family for the hospitality and helping me look great. I am grateful for that," Lieutenant Travis says.

Katja smiles. "Oh, Ma'am, I was glad to do it," she says. "We will have to have you over again. Maybe next time, we can also see this handsome young man from the ADA."

Lieutenant Taylor smiles. "Oh, I've got to get," she says. "I got to go pick up Lieutenant Young and show her around. Thanks again."

Rick walks through the motor pool as he heads to his office. He passes by the deadline row to his right and then opens the door to the building. Rick walks down the hall and enters his office.

Lieutenant Moore has his head in his hands, as he reads the maintenance reports. Rick walks over and sits next to Lieutenant Moore. He senses that he is frustrated.

"Sir, what's going on?" Rick asks.

"Oh, Sergeant First Class Taylor," Lieutenant Moore says as he sets the reports down on the table. "I head off with the Sawyers to Garmisch this weekend. I am ready to get it behind us if you know what I mean."

"I do, Sir. I really do," Rick responds. "About when are all of you heading out?"

"Well, we are trying to hit the road after lunch," Lieutenant Moore says.

"Go, Sir, we got everything under control here," Rick responds. "No one will know you are gone. You will get down there this evening and have Friday to Monday to have fun. Why not?"

Lieutenant Moore smiles "Thanks, Sergeant First Class Taylor, I appreciate it."

Katja is packing up, ready to go home for the day. Before she leaves, she stops by Rick's office to see if everything is good.

Rick waves at her, "I'll be home soon," he says.

She then walks down to Lieutenant Travis's office to check in on her. She can see Lieutenant Travis talking to Lieutenant Young through the window. Katja walks in, hoping to be just a moment.

"Melanie, this is Staff Sergeant Taylor. She is the best sergeant in the unit by far," Lieutenant Travis explains.

"Nice to meet you, Staff Sergeant Taylor," Lieutenant Young says while extending her hand.

"Nice to meet you as well, Ma'am, so what made you come to the army? Weren't you in the Pharmacy business?" Katja asks.

"Oh, my father is. I got my degree in the field. After living around it my whole life in the Pharmacy field, I wanted to come to Europe, and this was my chance," she explains, laughing as she speaks. "Can you imagine being a Logistical Officer for the army did the trick?"

"I guess whatever it takes, right Ma'am," Katja replies.

"Yep, I wanted to live here for a couple of years, not just visit here, and this was the way to do it," Lieutenant Young says.

Katja looks at her watch and replies, "oh, I got to get; good talking to you both. Lieutenant Travis, you look fabulous."

Katja's cell phone buzzes while she drives but she waits until she gets home to look at it. She pulls into the driveway, parks the car, and checks the messages. It says, "Franz," on the screen. She gets out of the car and goes inside.

Sabine greets her as she walks in.

"Hallo Katja, I hope you had a good day at work. How did Casey look?"

"Oh, she looked fabulous," Katja replies. "I got a buzz from Franz."

"Yes, I know," Sabine replies. "I think around eight tonight at the same place. I have supper ready for everyone; I'll just wait on Rick."

"Sounds good. Thanks, Sabine," Katja replies. "I will go upstairs and just check on the kids while I wait on Rick."

Sabine nods and smiles as Katja heads upstairs. When she reaches the top, she heads to Emma's room.

"Emma, so tell me about this boy, Randy," Katja says as she enters the room.

"Mom, he is so nice, he has these gorgeous blue eyes, and he always says the coolest things," Emma gushes.

"Does he treat you nice?" Katja asks.

"Yes, Mom, he has never been mean, to me," Emma tells her.

"So, he's a good guy," Katja confirms. "Good because your dad would not like you being a girlfriend to someone that wasn't great."

Downstairs, Katja can hear the front door open and Rick walking in.

"Hey Katja, check your phone, my love," Rick yells out.

"Oh, I am upstairs with Emma," Katja yells in reply.

Sabine comes around the corner by the kitchen and smiles at Rick.

"Okay, everyone, supper is ready. Wash your hands and come on down," she calls out to the rest of the house.

The kids all come running down.

After dinner, Rick and Katja start their familiar stroll down the Main River, heading to the Old Bridge. They take their time because they realize that they are leaving earlier than usual. Rick looks at Katja as they walk and smiles.

Katja smiles back and says, "don't stare too long; people may think we are lovers or something."

"You don't stare too long in my blue eyes," Rick retorts. "They are mesmerizing, and you may very well fall into the river."

Then Rick grabs her on the shoulder and pushes her in the chest to scare her and laughs.

Katja lets out a gasp. Then she punches him. "I don't think that is funny, Rick Taylor," she says.

They both look up towards the bridge as they approach and can make out that oh-so-familiar silhouette of Franz and his smoke at the center of the bridge.

They walk up the bridge and Rick can smell the aroma from Franz cigar.

"Hallo, my friends. It is good to see you," Franz says as they reach the center of the bridge.

"It is good to see you, Franz," Rick replies.

Katja nods in agreement.

Franz then says, "okay, you know the drill, I need you to watch both sides."

Katja responds, "We got it."

When they are all in position, Franz begins filling them in on what is new.

"To start it off, we got some information on the six," Franz explains. "We have found out three of them live here in Kitzingen. Two live in Würzburg, and one lives in Sulzfeld, a town south of us. The rest we still don't know. We know the one they keep referring to as The Mixer or 'the maker of toxic liquid.' They use those references a lot, and we think they are interchangeable in who they are referring to. We don't know if that person is male or female, or even what nationality they are. There is a lot to take in, so I will focus on the three that live here. Although, I will briefly cover each."

"Sounds good," Rick responds.

Then Katja interrupts. "We do have someone coming," she says as a figure comes into view.

Franz quickly changes the subject.

"So, how are the kids doing in school?"

"They are doing alright," Rick responds. "They enjoy it here. We have a son that has a little girlfriend, and the daughter has a little boyfriend too it seems."

Franz smiles and then takes a puff on his cigar as the person disappears around the corner.

"Okay, they passed by, so we are good now," Rick says.

Franz continues. "Well, the two who live in Würzburg are Russian. One is a man, and the other is a woman. Their names are Sasha Popova, and the guy is Pasha Stephenov. They live within a few blocks of where Hermann lived. Sasha and Pasha are not necessarily a couple, but they are part-time lovers, to put it nicely, more when it is convenient. They both seek other partners, it seems. Sasha has worked various jobs in Würzburg. Anything ranging from the clubs to waitressing and so on. On the other hand, Pasha has worked steadily for the same place for some time now, which is a butcher shop in downtown Würzburg. Now, there is the Polish woman. Her name is Gizela Gorski, she lives and works in Sulzfeld. Gizela works for a honey maker and lives down the street from the business. That is all I can tell you about those three, except we know that Sasha and Pasha both have sickle tattoos on their necks as well."

Rick and Katja nod in understanding.

"Someone is coming from my side," Rick whispers quickly.

"So do you have American TV at your house, or do you have just traditional German TV?" Franz asks.

"Just the traditional German TV," Katja replies.

"I like the weather channel early in the morning," Rick chimes in, smiling.

Franz smiles. "Most men do. It gives us a reason to get up early," he replies.

"They don't have a weather channel for the ladies, I see," Katja chimes in.

"I guess Germany has not evolved as much as we thought," Franz replies.

"We are clear," Katja says after checking the surroundings.

Franz picks back up where he stopped.

"Okay, the local people. We have three here; two on the east side of the river and one on your side of the river," he says. "Let's start with the one we have the most on. That is Andreas Lange. We know he lives in Kitzingen in the apartment complex on the east side of town in apartment 26. He has worked over at Sell Recycling GmbH & Co. along the Main River for years. His mom was in the Red Army Faction along with Andreas Baader. Her name was Gudrun Ensslin, and she was Baader's girlfriend. Many believe that Baader was Lange's father. He was raised by his uncle, who always said his last name was Lange. Andreas Lange has no current living relatives. Baader and Ensslin died in jail by a suicide pact, both members of the Red Army Faction. Baader and one other member died by gunshot wounds. Ensslin died by hanging. A fourth person who survived was believed to have stabbed herself in the chest four times. She has always claimed that it was not suicide and she did not stab herself. Instead, she claims her friends were executed by the state and she managed to survive the execution. Of course, Lange is believed to be named after who everyone thinks was his father, Andreas Baader."

"Wow, this dude has some deep baggage with this," Rick butts in.

"It would seem so," Franz replies. "Andreas has a sickle tattoo on one side of his neck and red RAF on the other side."

"So, this guy is all in, I presume," Rick says.

Franz nods his head in agreement.

"Andreas is one we have the most traffic on saying he has to meet with the mixer. We don't know if he is the leader, but if he is not, he is close to being the leader. Andreas is roughly 5 foot 9 and about 185 to 190 pounds. He is about 34 years of age, with blond hair and blue eyes, and he does tan easily."

Katja steps in. "This is like Rick said. It is deep."

Franz nods and blows out a puff of smoke.

"Then we have two others that we know a little about. Lena Klein lives at 23 Mainbernheimer Strasse on the first floor and is a nurse at Klinik Kitzinger Land. She is 5 foot 5, weighs about 125 to 130 and her hair color is the flavor of the week. It has been blonde, pink, blue, etc. She also has a neck tattoo of the sickle, and she is 28 years old. She has brown eyes and tan skin. Finally, we have Otto Braun, German Sharp Sickle works at the Globus Baumarkt, a hardware store in Kitzingen, and lives on Rosenstrasse 12 apartment 2. Otto is a larger fellow. He is over 6 feet tall and weighs about 230 pounds. Otto is in his mid-30s. He has a sickle tattoo on his neck also, and he has a bald head, wears earrings, and has brown eyes. Otto's skin is light. We are finding out more about these two. A few things we know is that they like to link up at Andreas' place a couple of times a month. They also like the club scene. They have been a sleeper cell for some time, so they did have everyday lives and a secret life. Let us focus on the Kitzingen crew. We know where they work, and we know where they live. Now I just got to get their habits, and we will probably use you two as well for surveillance on them. We must find out who the mixer is. Then we either terminate the mixer or prevent the desired attack. Unfortunately, the only real thing we know is that there is a desire to poison a major world player. We don't know if that establishes credibility or achieves the desired objective," Franz explains.

"That's a lot of information," Rick replies.

"Yes, it is," Franz replies. "I will send more information with some photos to look at. Those will go directly into my hands and to Sabine's hands. I don't want those out there loose."

"Yep, we got it," Katja replies. "When should we expect to do something again?"

"I would like to get you at least observing them by Saturday," Franz says. "All six are important, but I think if we start with Andreas, and Lena. We may squeeze Otto in as well."

"Okay sounds good, Franz," Rick responds.

Franz smiles, "you will hear from me soon."

Rick and Katja start to walk back home. They have already left the bridge and are almost home when Rick looks at Katja and says, "we need to watch our conversations on the walk; everything is really too close here. I suggest we keep conversations to the basement, the car, or someplace like the running field at work."

Katja nods her head in agreement, "I thought you wanted to talk about how you're walking with one hot mama along the river," she says with a smirk.

Rick smiles and kisses her. "Those are things we don't talk about with our words; we just use our actions, and I don't know why you still have those clothes on."

A big cheesy smile comes over Rick.

Katja then smiles in a flirtatious grin and chimes in. "Well, my, hmmm, objective, that will be when we get home, but only if you think you have the right stamina for this hot lady."

Rick and Katja make it home and go upstairs to their bedroom. As they are getting ready for bed, Katja looks at Rick and asks, "Rick, what about this guy Otto? Does he sound like he may be too much for you in a fight and such? Are you worried?"

"Not at all," Rick responds. "A man that size will not be as fast as me, and he will wear out quickly."

Then he smiles, forms a gun with his hand and says, "If the worst case, a simple pew pew will work."

Katja shakes her head. "Sometimes you're just too dumb, my love."

"Well, from what I understand, you like them dumb, I mean Kristoff, then Hermann, and who knows who else?" Rick replies.

Katja laughs. "That's right, the list is long, my love. They just keep coming out of the woodwork."

"So, when does the husband get on the list?" Rick asks. "Isn't there some fringe benefits to being your husband?"

Katja smiles and replies as she touches her face, "I am equal to all, my love, but I will make an exception just for you. So why don't you kiss your little spy girl wife?"

Rick wraps his arms around her waist and grabs her butt to pick her up and kisses her as they fall to the bed.

FRIDAY AT WORK

*I*t is the last day of the workweek, and Katja is excited. She is ready to not think about the Army so much. There is a lot on her plate coming up with the new missions, and she feels anxious. When she arrives at the base, Katja walks into her office and picks up the schedule of events for the day.

Rick arrives at work to find that Lieutenant Moore took his advice and called out for the day. So, without Lieutenant Moore, there will be no significant distractions. *I can focus on my work,* he thinks to himself, until Katja stops by his office. She looks around and notices that it's just her and Rick.

"So sexy man, where is everyone?" she flirtingly asks.

Rick smiles. "Well, it's just me here today, all by myself."

Katja grins and walks over to him. "Why don't you kiss a soldier?" she says as she walks over to him.

"Who am I to argue with that," Rick responds.

She leans over to kiss him as the office door opens and Lieutenant Young walks in. Katja and Rick quickly step away from each other casually. Lieutenant Young looks at both of them, not really noticing what was happening.

"Hey Sergeants, what's going on?" she says nonchalantly. "I am looking for Lieutenant Moore or Lieutenant Sawyer. Have you seen them?"

"Ma'am, they are on a pass right now," Rick responds. "Can I help you with something?"

"No, I don't think so," Lieutenant Young replies.

"Lieutenant Travis is in her office," Katja suggests.

"No, I don't need her. She has a big date tonight, from my understanding," Lieutenant Young responds.

She then walks out the door. Rick and Katja look at each other a little puzzled.

"What was that about?" Rick asks.

Katja shakes her head. "I have absolutely no idea."

She then leans over to Rick, gives him a quick kiss, and smiles. "I had to do that before someone comes back."

Rick smiles. "Oh, I am sneaking out around lunch today," Katja says. "I got some errands I need to run. I will see you later when you get home."

"Okay, I'll see you then," Rick replies.

Katja returns to her office and finds Lieutenant Travis there waiting for her.

Katja smiles. "Hey Ma'am, how are you? Are you ready for tonight?" she asks.

Katja can tell that Lieutenant Travis is buzzing with excitement. "Staff Sergeant Taylor, I am so ready for this evening," she says. "I've been waiting all week for tonight. It is going to be fun."

"Is there any certain place y'all are going to?" Katja asks.

Lieutenant Travis smiles. "He talked about going to a Winefest and then hanging out," she says.

"That should be fun," Katja replies. "But don't spend too much time drinking all the wine at the fest. Save some of that, hmm, energy for later," she says with a wink to Lieutenant Travis.

Lieutenant Travis blushes and then blurts out, "Oh, I got to get, but I will talk to you after this weekend. Is that good?"

"It sure is, Ma'am; go have fun," Katja responds.

Lieutenant Travis runs down the hall and disappears around the corner. Katja finishes some paperwork in her office. She looks around and thinks to herself; *I am about to call it a day here.*

Katja makes her way out the gate and decides to run by a couple of stores before heading home. She stops by the local drug store that is close to her house. As she pulls up, she notices Lieutenant Young wearing civilian clothes walking out of the drug store with two bags. *That is strange,* she thinks to herself. *Lieutenant Young has only been here a week. Soldiers get their pharmacy stuff for free on the post. Why would she be here at the local drug store on the economy? How would she even know about it?* Then she thinks back and remembers that Lieutenant Young's father is a pharmacist, and she went to school in pharmaceutical sciences. *But how would she know all about this already in less than a week? How is she getting around?* Katja gets out of her car and starts walking up to the drug store, but Lieutenant Young has already gotten into a car with someone, and they are about to speed off. Katja decides to worry about Lieutenant Young later as she enters the store and begins her shopping. She finds some new bath discs that are in different fragrances. They are used to place behind the back and fizzing once they hit the water to form a massage. She figures Rick would like them to soothe his back from time to time and decides to purchase them.

After leaving the pharmacy, Katja goes by the bakery and picks up some Kaiser Brötchen and a few other kinds of bread. Then she heads home. Along the way, she sees a lot of kids running the streets, just enjoying life. *They don't seem to have a care in the world,* she thinks. Watching these kids' innocence puts her in a pleasant mood as she pulls up to her house. She goes inside and hears Sabine in the house singing a German song.

Katja sneaks up on her. "Hallo, my Sabine, how are you doing?"

Sabine jumps and grabs her chest, saying, "I am doing fine, and you?"

Katja is smiling.

"Oh, Franz dropped this envelope for you and Rick to look through tonight," Sabine tells her. "It sounds like you two will have a reading date tonight?"

"That doesn't seem like much fun," Katja frowns.

"No, it doesn't," Sabine replies. "But time studying this will prepare you."

Katja nods in agreement.

"Well, you have all night on this, so don't get in a hurry," Sabine suggests.

Katja thinks for a moment then says, "you know what? Tonight, I will take my man out to the Greek restaurant and bring him home and maybe bed him well, then we will review the packet."

Sabine smiles. "That sounds like a good plan," she replies. "You know Spider-Man 2 is showing up on the hill at Larson. Maybe I'll take the kids out of the house to see that while y'all are having fun."

"Would you?" Katja asks gratefully.

"Certainly," Sabine confirms. "I'll take them downtown to a pizzeria, and we will walk it off with the hill on base to the theater in Larson."

Katja's eyes light up, and she hugs Sabine. "Thank you so much."

"No problem," Sabine replies. "Put this folder by your bed, so you don't forget."

Katja nods and starts to head upstairs.

"I'll get the kids out of here now before Rick arrives home," Sabine calls after her.

Katja looks back and says a quick thank you before continuing up the stairs.

She can hear Sabine calling all of the children into the kitchen as she walks up to her room with the packet.

When Rick arrives home and pulls up to the house, he doesn't see much movement with the kids or anyone. *That's odd,* he thinks to himself.

He opens the front door to a quiet house.

"Hello, is anyone home?" he calls out.

He doesn't get a response. He goes upstairs and looks around. Then he opens the bathroom door and finds Katja in the bathtub, leaning back with bubbles overflowing.

When she sees him standing in the doorway, she seductively sticks her leg out of the bubbles to tease him.

"Is there something you are looking for?" she asks

A smile comes across Rick's face as he says, "just an easy spy woman, that's all."

"It seems you may have found her, fella," Katja says confidently. "Why don't you come in here and see how easy she is?"

Rick immediately starts taking off his clothes.

"Stop! Stop! Be a little more romantic my love," she says while batting her eyelashes.

Like a good soldier, Rick follows orders pretty well. He begins slowly taking his clothes off. Katja claps as he removes each piece of clothing.

As the last piece of clothing hits the floor, Rick is finally naked. Katja looks at him with hunger in her eyes. "Why don't we have dessert first tonight, and later we can go eat? Get your butt in here."

When Rick is fully submerged in the tub and Katja says, "close your eyes."

He closes his eyes; she pulls out one of the fizzy massage discs that she bought for him and places it behind his back.

He jumps in surprise when it starts bubbling.

"What is that?" he asks.

"Oh, my love, it will make you feel great," Katja replies. "Just keep your eyes closed."

Rick can feel the disc fizzing as Katja turns around and leans back against his chest.

Once she is settled, Katja reaches behind her lower back, slowly grabs Rick's man parts, and asks, "how does that feel, my love?"

Rick hesitates and says, "my back feels great."

Katja turns around and tosses some water in Rick's face. He laughs and slides back but she pulls assertively on him to keep him under control. "Let's make love, Rick," she says abruptly.

Rick gets serious after that as they enjoy the bath as well as each other's body and affection. Rick picks up Katja, steps out of the bathtub and starts to take her upstairs.

"Stop!" Katja yells. "We are going to have water everywhere."

Rick follows her orders and puts her down.

Katja then over exaggerates bending over in front of him and rubs her butt on his stiffness as she grabs a towel. Rick smiles as they dry off and they then go upstairs. As they walk, Rick slaps Katja on the buttocks for every step she takes. This makes her walk slower and with more swings in her walk. Once they get into the bedroom, Rick starts to push Katja to the bed, and she stops him. Katja turns them around together and pushes him on to the bed. Rick smiles with anticipation. Katja climbs on top of Rick and starts gliding her body over his.

Afterwards, Rick and Katja lay in each other's arms for a bit, and then Katja says, "my love let's go eat. We are going to eat some Greek food tonight at the Akropolis."

"That sounds really good," Rick says.

Katja then looks at Rick.

"You know when Franz briefed us, he told us that big guy, Otto, lives down on the same street the Akropolis is on," she says.

"You are looking for another man tonight, my love?" Rick asks jokingly.

Katja slaps him on the chest.

"No, you were enough between my legs tonight, but just tonight," she says with a smile.

Rick then says, "in all seriousness, he lives that close."

"Rick in all seriousness, he is two doors down," Katja says. "We should make sure we walk by there as we go to the Akropolis."

Rick stops to think for a second. "Oh, my goodness, that is crazy how close he is to where we are going to eat. Maybe as we get close to the restaurant, we put a little separation between us, so he won't think we are a couple. That might come in handy later," he says.

"I agree," Katja replies. "When we get about a quarter mile away, I will lead, and you walk behind me about 200 yards in a loner way."

She chuckles as she says that and then goes on. "Oh also, we have a packet from Franz we have to review. I figure we would do that when we get back."

"No, I think we need to do that now, especially if we may be close to this guy," Rick replies. "We wouldn't want to screw this up."

Katja nods, agreeing. She is still naked as she picks up the folder and hands it to Rick who is sitting in his underwear. They go through the folder, laying the contents out on the bed.

The information focuses mainly on Andreas, Otto, and Lena. It provides photos that match Franz's description of them. There is a police photo of Otto and Lena that shows them with other body tattoos and four or five images of Lena with different hair colors. There is a page where Andreas refers to the mixer often and says that he doesn't get to see the mixer enough, or at least not as much as he would like. There is mention of an upcoming meeting at Andreas' place, supposedly on Sunday at around two in the afternoon.

"Franz put in here on the sheet the meeting time and location," Rick says. "That would be a good time for us to scope out the apartments for Otto and Lena or move to Würzburg and scope out Sasha and Pasha. Gizela is even an option, but Franz suggested that we start close first."

"Rick, what do you think of this?" Katja asks.

"The photos are very helpful, but also, we have a meeting location," Rick responds. "I agree we can probably get some intel off their places while they have their meeting. Franz is right; we should focus on Otto and Lena's places."

Katja nods her head in agreement. "Maybe we should find a different restaurant?"

Rick nods his head and smiles. "Yeah, I agree or maybe all we have tonight is dessert and no supper."

"Uh, no," Katja replies. "If you take me out, handsome man, then maybe we will have a second dessert."

Rick gets up and starts putting his clothes on, but Katja is still sitting there naked, looking at him. Rick stops dressing and looks at his wife.

"Oh, you mean now?" he asks.

Katja laughs. "No, my love, just thought I'd mess with you. Let's go get a Döner."

Rick smiles. "Sounds good, my love."

A NEW FRIEND

The next morning, Sabine wakes up and walks to the kitchen. She puts the coffee pot on and does a few things around the kitchen, then goes and takes a shower. As she gets out of the shower, she hears the doorbell ring. Sabine puts on her robe, still rubbing her hair with a towel, and walks to the front door. Sabine opens the door to find a boy standing there with blond hair and blue eyes.

The boy looks up and says in a deliberate tone, "Hello, I would like to play with Sebastian."

A bit surprised by his directness, Sabine looks at the young boy.

"What is your name, Mr. Early Bird?" she asks.

The young blond boy looks at Sabine. "My name is Lukas," he says. "Are you Sebastian's Mom?"

Sabine looks at him, chuckles for a second, then smiles at his precious innocence. "No, no, no. Come on now. Where do you live?"

"Oh, I live across the tracks by Globus Baumarkt," Lukas replies.

Sabine smiles with admiration as Lukas speaks perfect German. "One minute, please, let me get Sebastian," she replies.

Sabine tells Lukas to take a seat in the kitchen while she gets Sebastian.

Sabine walks upstairs to Sebastian's room, goes over to his bed and rubs his hair.

"Sebastian," she says quietly while running her hands through his hair.

He slowly begins to move, not wanting to get up.

Sabine continues to run her hand through his hair and says, "Sebastian, you have a friend. Lukas here for you."

Sebastian's eyes open and he jumps up. "Really?" Sebastian asks excitedly.

Sabine smiles, "yes, Sebastian."

Rick wakes up and walks down to the kitchen. He notices a boy that is not his sitting in his kitchen. Rick smells the aroma of coffee filling the room and goes over to get a cup.

Then he sits down by the boy. "How did you get in here?" he asks.

Lukas looks at him and says, "the pretty lady in the robe."

Rick thinks for a second, and he asks, "Whose boy, are you?"

"Mein Mama and mein Papa's," Lukas replies.

Rick thinks about the answer he just got from this young man. He thinks it is funny that the boy answered with no proper names, just his Momma and Papa. Rick keeps an observant eye on him.

Sebastian walks into the kitchen and exclaims, "Lukas!"

Lukas leaves the conversation with Rick and runs to Sebastian. Then they both run upstairs and start playing. Sabine walks in wearing her white robe and her hair still wet.

"Good morning, Sabine," Rick says. "Wow, that young man is early."

"Guten Morgen Rick, yes, he is," Sabine says. "I was just getting out of the shower when he rang the doorbell."

Rick gets up and pours Sabine a cup of coffee. "Here you go."

Sabine takes it and inhales the aroma. She rolls her eyes to embrace the aroma. "Danke," she says after she takes a sip. Then she says, "the boy, Lukas, says he lives over by the Globus Baumarkt. I wonder how Sabastian knows him."

"I don't know," Rick said.

Sebastian comes downstairs and runs up to Rick.

"Dad, we are going to the playground on our bikes is that okay?"

"No problem," Rick smiles. "But be home by lunchtime, okay?"

"Okay, Dad," Sebastian replies.

Lukas waves to Rick and Sabine as he follows Sebastian out the door.

Sabine looks at Rick. "Well, I will go get dressed. I'll be back down in a few."

Rick smiles and says, "yep, I got to go take a shower, then we are observing today."

"You two be careful," Sabine replies.

"Always," Rick replies.

Rick goes upstairs and crawls under the blanket with Katja.

"Hey, my love, it's time to wake up."

Katja just groans. Rick then places his cold hands around her waist and under her breasts.

Katja screams from the shock.

"Rick, dang it," she shouts.

"I love it when you scream my name, my love," Rick replies with a smirk.

"What do you want?" Katja asks in a groaning voice.

"Oh, we have some surveilling to do today," Rick answers.

"But it is my day off," she responds. She then rolls over and puts the pillow over her head.

"Spy work never ends, my love," Rick whispers.

Rick takes his shower and then makes his way back to the kitchen. Next, Katja finally migrates to the bathroom and starts taking her shower.

Sabine walks into the kitchen. "I will have you two some snacks and such for today," she tells Rick.

"Thanks, Sabine," Rick replies.

Katja walks into the kitchen, dressed and ready to go. "Are you ready?" she asks.

"Yes, I guess so" Rick responds.

SURVEILLANCE

They both wave bye to Sabine and get in the car. Rick looks at Katja and notices she has put on a pair of aviator sunglasses.

"Sunglasses, huh?" he asks sarcastically.

Katja smiles. "Yes, sunglasses, my love. We have to be incognito. Is that not how it is done?"

He shakes his head as he cranks the car. Katja leans over and puts a disc in the CD player and turns up the volume. The music comes out of the speakers and Rick looks at her as the theme music for *Mission Impossible* plays. He shakes his head again. Katja then hits the next selection and Rick waits patiently. The music comes out of the speakers playing the theme music to *James Bond* while Katja bobs her head to the music and takes it all in. She looks at Rick and attempts to talk in a British accent.

"Taylor! Rick Taylor, let's proceed."

Rick laughs and turns to her with his Bond voice.

"My dear, it seems you're enjoying this a bit."

"Rick, where are we going first?" Katja asks as they start driving.

Rick looks over at her.

"I thought you planned this," he says.

Katja smiles and says, "no, I am only good for being a sex object, not planning."

"Well, my love," Rick says in a false British accent. "You are quite well at that, if I do say so, myself." He smiles then goes back to his normal voice and says, "Okay, we will need a plan on this."

"Let's go to the Globus Baumarkt and see if we can simply see this Otto guy, and then we will go from there," Katja suggests.

"Sounds good," Rick agrees.

Rick turns at the intersection that takes them to the Globus while Katja watches the people walking along the street and the houses with lovely flowers on their windowsills. They arrive at the parking lot, and Rick pulls the car in between a few other cars where they can observe the entrance.

"Why don't I go in and have a look-see while you observe the parking lot," Rick suggests.

"Sounds good," Katja says. "Oh, do we have anything to eat?"

"Yep, Sabine made us some snacks," Rick replies.

"Cool, got to love Sabine," Katja replies.

Rick heads across the parking lot and enters through the green doors. He sees a few workers there but no one bald or over six feet tall. Rick checks the garden area and notices a young lady working there. He makes his way over to the lumber area. A couple of guys work there. Rick walks over to the electrical department, and no sign of Otto. He is beginning to think this is going to be boring.

Katja sits in the car and looks around as people walk into the store. One by one, people stroll into the Globus. Just ordinary people that want to improve their house and live their lives. She sees a few people shopping by themselves and a few couples, but mostly men entering the store. *I don't see much out of the ordinary out here, just people buying things they need,* she thinks.

Rick makes his way to the paint department. As he passes an aisle, he notices someone that looks familiar. When she looks over, Rick sees that it is Lieutenant Young.

"Hey Ma'am, what are you doing here?" Rick asks.

She turns to face Rick.

"Oh, Sergeant First Class Taylor, right?"

"Yes, Ma'am," He replies.

"You are married to Staff Sergeant Taylor, aren't you?" Lieutenant Young asks.

Rick nods yes.

Lieutenant Young steps closer to him. "Lieutenant Travis tells me she is a rock star," she says.

Rick smiles and says, "that would be correct."

He takes a quick look at what is in her cart, and sees that it is a can of turpentine.

"Ma'am what brings you here?" Rick then asks.

Lieutenant Young smiles. "Oh, just getting the essentials."

"Are you still in temporary quarters?" Rick asks.

"Oh yes, just for a few more weeks, then I will finally have an apartment," Lieutenant Young says.

Just then, a man walks around the corner. He is tall, very thick-built, and bald. He smiles and speaks German in a deep Bavarian accent directly to Lieutenant Young.

"Can I help you with something?" the man asks.

Lieutenant Young smiles as she responds in perfect German and touches the man's arm.

"No, Otto, I have what I need, maybe next time."

Rick is a bit surprised by Lieutenant Young. He notices a sickle tattoo on his neck as well as his nametag. Otto then has a disappointed look on his face and walks away.

Rick looks at Lieutenant Young. "Where and when did you learn German?"

"Oh, it's a long story; it would bore you," Lieutenant Young says. "It was nice seeing you, Sergeant First Class Taylor, but I do have to get. I got a lot of things to prepare for before tomorrow."

"You have a good day, Ma'am," Rick responds.

Rick continues to walk around the store for a few more minutes before heading back out to the car.

Katja is extremely bored in the car, but she notices two boys riding their bicycles, taking a shortcut through the Globus parking lot to some residential houses. She looks back at them and sees one is Sebastian. Katja is startled by this. *What is he doing over here?* She wonders. Katja looks back at the store and notices Lieutenant Young walking out.

Okay, Katja thinks, *she has been here a week already; been to the drug store on the economy, which would cost her money, and then to the hardware store. Does she even have an apartment yet?*

Rick taps the window and makes a face at her. Then he gets in the car.

"I just saw Sebastian riding his bike over here with another boy," Katja says.

"Oh yeah, he was supposed to go to the playground, not over here," Rick says. "The boy is named Lukas. He came by this morning while Sabine was getting out of the shower. I guess Sabine went to get Sebastian, and I went to the kitchen when I got up, and this boy was sitting in the kitchen. Anyway, Sebastian will be home by lunchtime."

Katja nods, listening. "Okay, and guess what else. I saw Lieutenant Young walk out of the store," she tells him. "She has only been here a week and has already ventured to the off-post drug store and the hardware store. Doesn't that sound strange, Rick?"

"It does but this will blow your mind," Rick replies. "I walked in there looking for Otto. I could not find him, and I found myself in the paint department. There is Lieutenant Young with a can of turpentine. What does a person who just got here need turpentine for? But that's not all. I chatted with her, and from around the corner, Otto walked up. He asked her if she needed help, and she answered him in perfect German. She called him Otto, as she knew him. It was on his shirt, but it was still like she already knew him, Katja. And she was touching his arm."

Katja's eyes grew big with excitement.

"You know her Dad is a pharmacist," she says. "She has a degree in pharmaceutical sciences, she buys two bags worth of stuff from the drugstore within a few days of arriving here and then she buys turpentine. Do you think she may be this mysterious mixer?"

Rick has a look on his face like he just had a revelation.

"Katja, I think you might be right. We need to discuss this with Franz."

"I agree but let's look at a few more people," Katja replies. "We know where Otto is right now, so let's just drive by his apartment. After that, we know Lena is a nurse. We probably won't get much from the hospital, so we can also just drive by her place. And Andreas' place is close to Lena's, so we can drive by his apartment, too. That way we have an idea of where they all live. Then after that, I suggest we go to Sulzfeld and check out the Polish honey lady. There we can act like we are in the mood for honey. What do you think?"

"Sounds good," Rick replies. "Let's go."

They start driving close to Otto's apartment.

"Oh, my goodness, that is only two doors down from the Greek restaurant," Katja says. "I am glad we didn't come by last night."

"Well, I was too, but not about the food," Rick smiles.

Katja snaps as she hits him and says, "Chut up!"

Rick smiles as he looks at the front door of the apartments in the old house.

"There must only be one entrance into the building and each apartment has its entrance once you are inside, it seems."

Katja nods in agreement.

They start driving to Lena's place. As they go through town, Katja asks, "can you believe this with Lieutenant Young?"

"It is crazy," Rick says.

Lena's apartment is not far from the Old Bridge, just on the other side of the river. The bridge is only used for walking, not driving, so it takes them a bit to get around it. As they pull up to Lena's place, they see that it is a small house that rents out two apartments on the inside. An ordinary family probably lives there, renting the other house areas out.

"This doesn't look too hard to get into," Rick says. "I just need to know which place is her's."

Katja nods.

"Let's drive by Andrea's place now," she says.

They pull up to the apartment and Rick is surprised how close the two locations are to each other.

"Wow, it was only a couple minute drive from Lena's place," he says.

"We know he lives on the second floor," Katja states. "Let's just see if we can walk in and check out the floors."

Rick is hesitant as Katja puts her sunglasses on.

"Come on, spy man," she says. "Let's go up to the doorbell selection list and see if we find his name, then let's try to walk the first or second floor."

"Okay, if we do this, we separate," Rick says. "You go to the doorbell selection, and I will walk by apartment 26."

"Yes!" Katja exclaims.

Rick looks at her seriously.

"We are back here no matter what in ten minutes, understand?"

"Party popper," Katja frowns. "Yes, my love."

Rick gets out of the car first and walks up to the door of the apartment complex. It is not locked so he walks in. As soon as Rick is in, Katja walks up to the entrance to look at the names on the doorbells. Rick moves up to the second floor and passes apartments 21 and 22. He sees someone come out ahead. He stops to look at his phone for a second and out of the corner of his eye, he sees a woman with pink hair. As she walks by, he notices a sickle tattoo on her neck.

He quickly sends a text to Katja.

Go back to the car now.

Then he walks down the hall and realizes that she came out of apartment 26. Rick walks past the apartment and notices the nameplate that says "Baader" on it. He looks around for a second and heads back downstairs. As he walks out the front door, he sees his car and Katja is sitting there.

Rick gets in the car and says, "just be cool till we get down the road."

When they get about half a mile down the road, Katja can't keep holding on to what she learned. "Rick, the name on the apartment complex was not Lange," she blurts out.

"I know it was Baader," Rick says.

"No," Katja replies. "The one down by all the doorbells had Ensslin on it. That is his mother's last name."

"Wow, because upstairs had Baader on it. That is his father's last name," Rick responds.

They look at each other. "That is some crazy shit," Katja says.

"Did you see the girl in pink hair come down?" Rick asks.

"Yes, why?" Katja says.

"That was Lena," Rick replies smugly proud that he knows something Katja doesn't. "She had the sickle tattoo and came out of Apartment 26 when I got up there. I sent you a text to get to the car."

"Shut the fuck up!" Katja replies excitedly. "I didn't notice the text. No fucking way. I saw the girl, and she looked at me and walked away. I just thought she was a bitch. Well, come to think of it, I may not be wrong on that."

Rick laughs and starts driving to Sulzfeld.

Katja looks over. "Rick, we have some interesting data today. Can you believe that?"

"No," Rick replies. "I seriously didn't think we would run into anyone today. I am surprised."

"Now, with Gizela Gorski, we don't know if she has a sickle tattoo or not," Katja says.

"We don't know anything except she works there," Rick replies matter-of-factly. "So, when we get there, we are a typical American family that wants to buy fresh honey."

Rick and Katja pull up to the store and walk in. They quickly realize that this is a pretty good size place and not your typical honey stand. The honey manufacturer produces honey for wine, lip balm, medicinal purposes, and some manufacturing commodities. An older man, who they assume is the owner, greets them from behind the counter.

Katja looks at him and gives him a smile in return.

"I am looking for some honey for lip balm and eating," she tells him.

"Gorski, come help these people, please," He yells in German.

At hearing the name Gorski, Rick looks at Katja.

A woman, about the age of 35, comes from the back of the shop. She is very slender and tall, probably around 5 foot 10. She may weigh at the most 135 lbs. She has dark eyes and long, straight blonde hair that runs down to the middle of her back.

The lady approaches Rick and Katja and says, "may I help you?"

"Yes, I am looking for lip balm and honey for the house," Katja replies.

Gorski then says, "follow me."

As they walk down the aisle, Rick notices that she is beautiful, but he does not see a neck tattoo.

She stops and says, "here is the lip balm. Would you like to sample it?" Gorski grabs a sample and puts it on her lips in almost a seductive way. "I use it on my lips a lot. It works better than any other lip balm. It is all-natural," she says.

Then she pops her lips and looks at Rick as she hands a sampler to Katja. Katja is not happy one bit about her actions. She takes it, rubs her finger on the lip balm, and then puts it on her lips.

"Oh my, it feels good," Katja exclaims.

Gorski continues to stare at Rick and suggests, "we also have honey wine which is good for those special evenings." She then turns to Katja and finishes her sentence. "And regular honey if you like."

At this point, Katja is fuming.

"I am going to get a couple of lip balms, one wine, and one honey," she says.

Gorski smiles at her.

"I will get all that for you and meet you up front," she says.

"Sounds good," Katja replies.

Katja pays for the honey products, and Gorski says, "Tschüss."

Katja responds back, "Tschüss."

Rick walks out with Katja and they get in the car. Rick cranks the car and starts to drive off.

"That bitch would've loved to put that lip balm on your lips if I wasn't there," Katja blurts out.

Dumbfounded, Rick says, "I thought she was nice."

Katja shudders.

"Of course, you do, Rick; you are a guy," she replies. "She already had lip balm on. She just wanted to show you that she knew how to put *things* on her lips. She wanted you to look at her."

Rick looks at Katja.

"Well, my love, obviously, you are way more receptive than I am," he says. "I never saw that at all. Now, if that was her intent, I surely missed it. I would have liked to notice that, but I didn't. If I am going to get gripped out about it, at least I could have noticed it. I was thinking out of all of them so far, if I had to kill her, she might be the hardest because she was so nice."

Katja gets even more mad at this.

"Don't worry about it. She will be the first one I kill," Katja shouts.

Rick tries to change the subject.

"Hey Katja, somewhere on this street she supposedly lives."

"I'll be here tonight," Katja replies.

Rick just shakes his head. "Why don't we give Franz a call, my love."

"The sooner, the better so I can claw her eyes out," Katja exclaims.

"Katja, why don't you give Franz a call so we can meet up?" Rick asks.

"Fine!" Katja replies angrily.

Rick and Katja drive back to their home. As they pull up to the house, they notice two bicycles there. Katja feels a buzz on her phone. It is Franz.

She looks at Rick and says, "Franz will be here in about 30 minutes."

Katja walks inside and notices a little blond boy playing in the living room with Sebastian.

"Who is this guy?" Katja asks.

"This is Lukas," Sebastian replies.

Katja then looks at Sebastian and says, "We saw you two over at the Globus."

With no care in the world, Sebastian says, "oh yeah, that is where Lukas lives."

Rick butts in. "Sebastian, we don't have a problem if you are going over there but if you do, let us know that, okay?"

"Yes, Sir," Sebastian replies.

Sabine walks into the living room from the kitchen.

"How was your day so far?" she asks Rick and Katja.

Katja looks at her. "Very enlightening," she tells her. "And Rick is not allowed at the honey store anymore."

Rick just shakes his head while Sabine gives a surprised look.

"Franz will be over soon," Katja says. "We will probably have him eat lunch with us."

"Oh yeah, that is fine," Sabine replies. "Michael is at Angelika's, and they are trying to go to the Kino later. Emma is downtown with Randy at the candy store, most likely. Jonas and Noah are over at Johannes's place. So, it is just us, Sebastian, and Lukas."

"Oh my, the Kino, that is expensive," Katja exclaims. "It is like 15 euros a person whereas, he could just go up the hill for $1.25."

Rick steps in and smiles.

"Only the good girlfriends get taken to the Kino; the others go on the cheap date to the post theater," he says with a smile.

SHARP SICKLES
APARTMENT PREPARATION

*A*fter lunch, Franz gets up from the table and looks at Sebastian.

"It is good to see you again, Sebastian, and it was nice to meet your friend Lukas," he tells the boys.

Both boys smile, and Lukas says, "Danke."

"Maybe we should go down to the basement," Rick suggests.

Franz agrees and starts down the stairs, with Katja and Rick following.

When they are all downstairs, they form a small circle in the middle of the room. They look back and forth between each other to determine who will go first. Finally, Katja speaks up.

"Well, we did a bit of surveillance today, Franz," she begins. "We saw a few members and we got some interesting information. First, the honey girl in Sulzfeld, I am okay with killing her now. She has eyes for Rick, and he doesn't want to admit it."

Rick sighs as he drops his head down and starts shaking it sideways.

Franz laughs. "There may be an opportunity for you, but let's stay focused on this first."

Katja smiles and nods in an agreeing way.

"Tell me what all you found out," Franz says.

"Well," Rick starts. "We went to each apartment in Kitzingen. We know where they are at, and on some, we can get in if we have the exact apartment number. We knew Otto was at work because we went there, and I saw him."

Franz tilted his head for a moment. "You saw him?"

"Oh yeah," Rick responded.

He tells Franz all about meeting Otto at the hardware store and their suspicions of Lieutenant Young.

After Rick is finished, Katja jumps in to tell him about the apartments and honey stand. When she is finished, Franz takes a moment to process all the information they had just told him.

"We have strong reasons already to believe the mixer is an American," Franz says thoughtfully. "We don't know if the mixer is male or female, but this is interesting."

Franz smiles, and Rick says, "so Franz, that is what we got today so far."

Franz looks at both of them.

"That is excellent work, guys. So, I got each of you an Olympus camera," he says as he pulls one out of each of his Jacket pockets. "The camera is a digital camera, so you don't need to worry about film. You will both need these to take photos. I suggest that until we know more, you keep doing missions together, not separately. Tomorrow at 1:30 p.m., I want you in a position where you can observe Lena leave her apartment. Once she leaves, you are to enter and find out everything you can. There will be no stealing, and you will only get about twenty minutes at the max for her place. You will take photos and try to leave the place as you found it. She is on the first floor, the first room on the right. Once you finish there, you will go to Otto's apartment. You will have twenty minutes there, as well. You have the same mission. He lives in apartment two, the second door on the right. Now, if for some reason anyone returns early, kill them. I expect both of you to bring a gun and Katja, that knife of yours."

Katja smiles a sadistic grin.

Rick shakes his head as he feels Franz is feeding her ego.

"No matter what if one shows up, you must terminate them, do we understand?" Franz says seriously.

Both Katja and Rick nod their heads in agreement.

"If that happens, phone me immediately, and we will go from there," he tells them.

Rick and Katja are silent for a moment.

Franz looks at Rick and Katja, then says, "try out the Olympus Stylus 300 cameras. You can simply erase a shot, but we will be able to download the photos. Once downloaded, we can even zoom in on the image and such. But after you play around with them, delete them all before going on a mission because the card in the camera goes off so much space it has."

"Sounds good," Rick replies. "We will be on point at 1:30 in the afternoon tomorrow."

Katja nods in agreement.

"Good," Franz replies. "My friends, we will be watching the Andreas house, and we will shoot you a text when they get out. From what we understand, their meetings or parties normally go for at least two hours. I will likely see you two tomorrow to retrieve some data."

The couple nods and then they all head back upstairs to see Franz off.

"Bye Franz," Katja says when they get to the front door. "Let me know when I can take the Honey Girl from Poland out."

Franz shakes his head. Rick waves at Franz.

APARTMENT SEARCHES

Katja wears comfortable jeans, a buttoned-up red blouse with a black Jacket and some sneakers for comfort and mobility. She has her T handle push dagger on the right-hand side in her belt loop. She has a large pocket inside her jacket on her left side where the gun is, and she has another large pocket on the right inside of her jacket for the camera. Rick is wearing jeans, running shoes, a black T-shirt, and a black jacket over the shirt to conceal his gun. He is wearing a simple shoulder harness, and the Beretta is on his left side.

At 1:20, they get in the car and drive to Lena's apartment. They park a block down from her apartment to see someone leave the apartment.

Rick leans over to Katja.

"You sure don't want to go to Sulzfeld and buy some more honey, my love," he teases.

"Rick, don't you start on me," Katja warns. "We will go over there and kill Ms. Lip Balm right now, and I won't even think twice about it."

"I just wanted to get your juices going, that's all," Rick says.

"Funny," Katja replies. "Do you see me doing that, haha hehe thing?"

"Katja, up ahead," Rick then says. "Ms. Pink Hair, Lena walking towards Andreas' place. Let's give her a few minutes."

Rick and Katja get to the front door of Lena's apartment. Rick picks the lock, and Katja walks in with Rick following behind her as she shuts the door. In front of them is an area for shoes and coats, and a thin door that opens up into a split area of the apartment. On one side is a living room and a kitchen, and on the other side is a small bedroom and a bathroom.

"Let's split up," Katja says. "I'll take the bathroom and bedroom." Katja winks at Rick as she says bedroom.

Rick agrees and moves on to the living room and kitchen.

In the living room is a small sofa and TV. Under the TV there are some books. A lot looks like some old German literature and maybe some Eastern bloc literature. *Nothing worthy of a photo,* he thinks. Rick goes into the kitchen. He pulls every drawer and doesn't find much.

"Rick come here," Katja calls.

Rick goes into the bedroom and sees a lot of papers by the computer. The computer is left on but has password security to it. Rick takes a photo.

On one piece of paper, a note is written.

The mixer needs to show up, damn Amerikaner.

Further down the page is another scribbled message.

Amerikaner from Harvey is finally ready for the toxic solution.

Rick takes a photo of the whole page. The second page has a drawing of the sickle on Lena's neck and has a list of names on it.

The list starts with a short paragraph.

Make them pay, any German that had any dealings with the killing of the RAF, make them pay. Gerhard Schröder and George W. Bush are a bonus.

Further down the page, it says,

Embarrass Germany by killing the American President on German soil. Sever the alliance.

Rick takes a photo of this page as well.

As he takes the picture, he looks further down the page and sees a date.

October 15th Schröder to stop in Würzburg for a speaking engagement along with President Bush.

Rick takes a close-up photo and realizes that it is about three to four weeks away. Then he looks at his watch and sees they still have a few minutes before they need to leave.

Katja is rummaging through Lena's drawers by her bed. She finds some photos of Lena naked with a guy who she assumes is Andreas. Rick takes pictures of those as well. Underneath the keyboard is a piece of paper with the password for the computer and a list of people. Besides, some of their names is a sickle, almost like a checkmark, as if to indicate those that are in a group or club. Rick wishes they had more time, but he takes a photo of the paper, and he also takes a picture of the computer system, including the serial number and model number in case someone needed to return and hack it. Katja makes sure they put everything back and nods to Rick while pointing at her watch. He nods yes, and they leave.

Rick and Katja pull up about 100 yards away from Otto's apartment. They make their way to the second door on the right and Rick picks the lock. Katja goes in first. Immediately they are in the living area with a kitchen to the side. There is a door straight ahead that leads to a bedroom with a bathroom attached to it. Rick goes through the living room and doesn't find much, just like the last place. The sofa is a modern black sofa. The TV and stand look very stylish. They both go to search the bedroom. Once entering the door, there are posters reminiscent of Eastern Europe. The bed has black satin sheets on it and an ashtray next to it with the ashes almost overflowing. At the end of the bed is some open space. In the far corner is a computer table and computer. Opposite to that is the door to the bathroom. Behind the door to the room is clothes Schrank (German wardrobe closet) which Katja opens to search. There are tons of clothes there and behind the clothes are some weapons that look like they came from a martial arts studio. There is also a box in the corner that has photos in it.

Katja turns to Rick. "It is hot in here. I am going to put my Jacket here for right now," she says. She then smiles and puts her hand on her face as she looks at Rick, "Oh, Rick, it is so hot in here, this has to come off."

Rick smiles but shakes his head in disagreement. Then he starts looking around the computer and the desks.

Katja pulls the camera out of her jacket that she set on the edge of the bed by the pillows. She looks through the photos from the closet. There are pictures of men and women without their shirts on. Each of them has a sickle tattoo on their neck. A few photos have the tattoos on their torso or arms instead of their neck. Most show their faces, but the ones with the tattoo on their torso or arms, the faces are cut off. *They must be trying to hide their identity,* she thinks. Katja takes a photo of each of the images. Katja finds a photo of Lena with her tattoo. This time, her hair is blue. She sees a picture of Rick's favorite person, the Honey Girl, and her tattoo is under her left breast. Katja finds a photo of Hermann naked as well. In all the photos, everyone is at least completely topless or naked.

Rick pulls open a drawer in the computer desk and says quietly, "Katja, come here now."

Katja walks over there to where Rick is standing, and she gasps. Rick is holding a set of enlarged photos. The first photo is a picture of Sebastian riding his bicycle by Globus.

Katja starts getting nervous.

"Rick, Rick, Rick, what the fuck is this?" she asks.

"Calm down, my love," Rick says.

Rick flips to the next photo and it is Emma on the moped with Phillip.

Katja is breathing heavily, and her heart is racing.

Rick remains calm and flips to the next picture. They both gasp again. It is a photo of Katja outside the Airport Club with Hermann.

Someone wrote above the photo. It reads-

Schwarze Witwe, Zauberin, Frau des Todes, Verführerin.

Rick looks at Katja as she gasps.

"What does that mean?" he asks.

Katja is breathing heavily and blurts out, "that fucker is calling me a Black Widow, an Enchantress, a woman of death, and Seductress," she translates.

The next photo shows Hermann kissing her and Katja grabbing his crotch. Then there are more photos of Katja in the club.

Katja holds her stomach.

"Those fuckers know our family."

Rick quickly takes photos of everything.

Katja and Rick both receive a text from Franz.

Otto has left early, be careful.

Katja is hysterical and runs into the bathroom where she vomits in the toilet. Rick starts looking through the rest of the desk to find more things to take photos of.

Otto arrives at the front door of the apartment. Both Rick and Katja are utterly unaware of his arrival. Otto quietly opens the door and walks into the bedroom. Rick's back is to him, Katja starts to step out of the bathroom, and she sees Otto.

"Rick!" She yells.

Otto lunges toward Rick and hits him in the back of the head as Katja is yelling. Rick collapses immediately to the ground and is out cold.

Katja looks at Otto and yells, "you mother fucker," as she runs to hit him.

Otto is far too large for her, and he catches her as she runs into him. His hands are around her throat, and he pushes her up on the wall next to the bathroom. Rick lies behind him between the bed and the computer.

Katja is swinging her arms franticly at Otto without much success.

Otto looks at her as he has her up against the wall with her feet off the ground

"So little seductress," he says. "Did you at least fuck my friend Hermann before you killed him, or are you just a tease? I saw you leave with him."

Katja is having a hard time breathing. Otto's giant hands are cutting off her airway and she realizes this.

He leans into her.

"Tell me, you little bitch? Did you fuck him at least?" he demands.

She starts kicking him several times in the legs and with each kick, he moves his body back from the wall. Katja finally gets the distance that she needs and kicks Otto in the stomach and the groin. As Katja lands the groin kick, Otto immediately weakens and falls back on the bed, still holding her around the neck, and she falls on top of him. Katja has lost her leverage of kicking from the position she is in. She starts hitting him with her fists. Otto fights her arms back and rips her blouse and sports bra off in one swipe. Katja's breasts are swinging as she swings but her blows are ineffective against Otto's strength. He manages to effortlessly roll himself and Katja over on the bed to get on top of Katja.

Otto looks at her.

"Well bitch, before I kill the little seductress, I will fuck you for Hermann, then I will fuck you for me."

He slaps her in the face. His hands are so large that it disorients her for a second. She slides her hand behind her back and rests her hand on the T handle push dagger. Otto starts to undo her pants and chuckles as he does it.

Katja grabs his pants to undo them with her left hand.

"Well, I am no tease," she says. "I am the real deal, so if you're going to fuck me, then fuck me and let's make it fun, don't make me break you."

Otto looks stunned for a second and pauses. He second-guesses the situation. Otto quickly looks over his back to make sure Rick is still down and that is all the distraction Katja needs.

She pulls herself up with her grip on his pants and thrusts the dagger into his neck with her right hand repeatedly.

"You watched my kid's, mother fucker. You spied on my kids. You fucked with my family, fucker. You fucked with the wrong woman," she screams with each stab.

Blood shoots across the room and onto Katja's face and chest as she hits Otto's arteries. Otto's eyes are in disbelief. Katja is still steadily stabbing his neck over and over. Rage and adrenaline fill her. Otto is weak but is also a lot of weight. He falls on top of her, still spewing blood and gurgling with every breath. With every ounce of energy Katja has, she rolls him over to where she is on top. As she does, she keeps on stabbing him. For Otto, this happened so quickly. It was over before he knew what had happened. Katja is on an extreme frenzy running on pure rage as she continues to stab Otto.

"Die, die, die," Katja shouts as she stabs.

Rick slowly starts to move. He hears a gurgling noise and someone yelling. It is Katja cussing.

Rick musters all his breath to get her attention.

"Katja," he gasps. "Katja... Are you... Okay?"

Katja finally stops stabbing Otto and jumps down and rushes to Rick. She is drenched with blood, and Rick is shocked when he sees her. He doesn't comprehend what he sees.

"Rick, my love," Katja yells. "Rick, are you okay?"

Rick's eyes are wide open in fear as he sees her with all the blood dripping off her.

"What happened, Katja?"

She is shaking with rage. Katja starts to speak, "that sorry, mother fu-"

She stops mid-sentence and turns to Otto. There is blood everywhere, but Otto moves slightly. Katja gets her jacket with blood all over it, pulls out her Beretta with the suppressor and points at Otto's head.

"Die, you bastard," she says as she pulls the trigger twice.

Smoke billows from the tip of her suppressor, brass casings swirl on the ground and the air fills with smell of gunpowder. Katja, behind her blood-soaked body, is the epitome of stoic.

Methodically, Katja pulls out her cellphone and calls Franz. Rick is slowly coming out of his confusion. He grabs the phone from Katja and listens. Katja still has blood dripping off her face, her chest, and her arms. She is covered with blood.

Franz answers the phone, "Hallo."

"Franz, we need help," Rick replies. "We've got a mess here, and we need a car at the door. Katja is covered in blood."

"Rick, are you and Katja okay?" Franz immediately asks.

"Yes, we are," Rick assures. "We don't look good right now, but we are okay. After we leave, we will need a mop-up crew."

"I am there in five minutes," Franz says. "Once I get there, I will give you a ring so you two can get out as discreetly as possible. The mop-up crew will be there about ten minutes after we leave."

"Sounds good," Rick replies.

Katja is still hovering over Otto with her pistol in hand.

After Franz hangs up, Rick calls Sabine. Sabine answers, "Hallo."

"Sabine, I need a few things," Rick begins. "I need the kids to be in the basement until I get Katja in the bathroom. Once we are there, I'll lock the door. We will need some clothes, and you will probably have to mop behind us. There is blood everywhere, but we are alright. Also, if you can have Katja's car moved so Franz can pull right up to the door to keep the neighbors from seeing. We will be there within ten minutes."

"Of course, it will all be taken care of," Sabine replies. "Are you two, okay?"

"Yes, we are," Rick replies.

"I'll see you in a few," Sabine replies.

Rick hangs up and looks around. He sees Katja still standing over Otto's dead body.

"Katja, my love," he says. "Get your jacket and keep it in your hand. Make sure you have the camera and the pistol. You are going to wear my jacket when we go outside. Do you hear me?"

"That mother fucker had pictures of Sebastian," Katja replies, her fury growing with every word. "That is our family, Rick. Call off the mop-up. Call off Franz. I will sit here until every one of them comes to check on Otto. I will fill this apartment with bodies."

"Katja, my love," Rick says in a soft, soothing voice. "I know, and we will kill them all if we have to, but right now, let's go home."

Katja slowly nods her head. She grabs her jacket and then puts Rick's jacket on. She looks at Rick.

"Rick, I love you. You know that, right?"

"Oh, I do, my love," Rick responds. "I am a lucky man. Me you too, my love, me you too."

The phone buzzes, and it's Franz. They slowly open the apartment door to see if anyone is in the hallway. No one is there. They move swiftly to the exit and Franz's car is there with the back door open. Rick quickly pushes Katja, and then himself, into the back seat, closes the door, and taps Franz's headrest.

"We are on cobblestone, so it will feel uncomfortable, but I'll have you home in a few," Franz says.

Franz pulls up to the house, and the door is already open. Rick ushers Katja upstairs quickly and Sabine follows them with the mop. Franz shuts his car off, makes a couple of phone calls and sits out on the second-floor balcony with his cigar. Franz checks his sidearm and sits in a way that he can keep watch over the Taylor house.

Sabine already had the water in the tub. She has a key to the bathroom and opens the door as Rick and Katja are taking their clothes off.

"Oh dear," Sabine gasps.

Rick turns to her and says, "lock the door behind you."

Sabine does. Then she walks over and turns on the shower that is separate from the tub.

"Guys," she says. "Let me take care of this. Just stay still. Katja, my friend, let me get your pants off."

Sabine pulls the pants and panties off as Katja places her hands on Sabine's shoulders. She guides Katja into the shower then turns to Rick.

"Just one moment," she tells him as she puts Katja's clothes in the sink.

He has a lot of blood on him, but it is from Katja holding him. The shower runs over Katja as she huddles next to the glass to let the water spray her.

Sabine looks at Rick and says, "Okay, Rick, your turn."

His shirt is already off, he unbuttons his pants, and she pulls them off along with his underwear. She notices Rick's privates out of the corner of her eyes. She takes a mental note and internally smiles. Sabine looks at him and says, "hold tight."

She goes to the shower with Katja and grabs the removable shower head. Katja just stands there while Sabine hoses her down thoroughly.

"Hold your arms up, so I get under your boobs," Sabine directs. Katja does as she is told and raises her arms.

"Oh, my goodness, there is a lot of blood there," Sabine exclaims. "Okay, spread your legs wider, there we go." Sabine sprays every body part that Katja has, and Katja simply cooperates with the commands. Then Sabine says, "Come, come, my dear." She puts Katja, and a massage disc, in the tub.

Sabine turns to Rick. "You're next," she says as she guides him in the shower.

"I can do this," Rick says.

"I got this," Sabine assures. "You are almost done anyway." She hoses him down.

"Go ahead lift your arms up," Sabine directs. "There we go. Okay, move your junk around. There we go." After she hoses Rick down, she turns off the shower.

"Come on join your wife. I will be back in a second," she says.

Sabine takes the clothes and checks every pocket, removing cameras, phones, money and guns, then she puts them in the washer. Sabine then returns to the bathroom, unlocks the door again, and walks in with two glasses of wine and the bottle.

"I thought you might need these," Sabine says. "The kids will be in the basement until you two get out. Your new clothes are on the toilet. Franz will have someone here all night. Right now, Franz hasn't moved from the balcony. He is watching diligently."

"Thank you, Sabine," Rick says.

Katja looks up from the bubbling bath water to Sabine.

"My family was threatened today, and I defended it," she says sternly. "Sabine, you, too, are part of the family. I would protect you like I would my own. Thank you."

Sabine walks away with a smile and locks the door.

Katja looks at Rick.

"Rick, we have a problem," she says, concern filling her voice. "If Otto knew Sebastian and me, then others may as well. How do we protect the kids fully? I can't believe I am even asking that with Sabine around. She is the perfect protector, but what about when they are with friends or at school. There is no other better protection than what we have, which is apparently not good enough. So how do we fix that?"

"Then what do we do?" Rick asks.

"The only way to protect them more than they already are protected is to tell them," Katja decides. "Then they will be vigilant. We must do this because now they will always be in harm's way. They are not like other school kids."

"Katja, this is crazy," Rick says. "But at the same time, this makes a lot of sense."

Katja leans over to Rick and kisses him.

"Rick, you do know, I killed a man today. I think that is in a song, really not sure," Katja says.

"I do, my love and I realize I wouldn't be here today if it weren't for you," Rick replies.

Katja stares into his blue eyes.

"My love, look deep into my eyes," she says, lifting his chin to meet her gaze. "I want you to know that I would kill every day for the rest of my life if that was what it took to keep looking into your blue eyes every day."

"Katja, do you understand what your eyes can do to a man?" Rick says, still looking at Katja.

Katja touches his face and leans in next to his ear. "Tell me, Rick," she whispers. "What do my eyes do?"

FAMILY DINNER

*W*hen the water starts to get cold, Rick gets out of the bathtub and grabs a towel for Katja. She stands up and jokingly grabs his penis.

"Uh oh. That's not the towel," she says with a smile.

Katja takes the towel, walks over to the wine bottle, and drinks about a third of it straight from the bottle. Then she turns to Rick.

"Let's go talk to Franz," she says, motioning to the door.

"Maybe we should get some clothes on first, don't you think?" Rick says.

"Well, I figured since Sabine is seeing you naked, why not Franz see me naked?" Katja jokingly asks.

"Wait, Katja, first Hermann sees you naked, Otto sees your boobs, and now you want Franz to see you naked? Are you getting side money for all this?" Rick jokes back.

"Wait now, Hermann never saw anything," Katja says defensively. "Now he did some touching, groping, and yes more touching with his you-know-what, but before he could see anything, someone shot him in the dick."

She takes a few steps toward Rick as she continues down the list.

"Now, Otto, that big beast, did rip my shirt off, but Mr. I Am Faster Than Him never showed up," she teases. "So, I had to kill him with my boobies jiggling."

She stops and thinks for a second.

"Okay, maybe Franz doesn't need to see me. I guess people die when that happens. Unless it's you," she says with a wink.

Rick laughs and shakes his head.

"Yeah, maybe we need to spare Franz his life," he says.

Katja hits him on the arm then looks around for a moment.

"Rick, I've got to tell you something," she says seriously.

Rick gives her his undivided attention.

"I am famished my dear," Katja says. "That adrenaline went right through me. I feel like I ran a marathon and haven't eaten in a year. I need some."

Rick raises an eyebrow and makes a sexual gesture. Katja rolls her eyes.

"No, not that," she says with a sigh. "I need food, dammit. I am starving."

"Well, let's finish getting dressed and see what Sabine has in the house as we talk to Franz," he suggests.

Rick opens the door. He looks to the right, and he can see out one of the kids' bedrooms to the balcony facing the street. There is an all too familiar silhouette of a man standing, smoking, and looking out into the night. He looks like a faithful sentry. It is Franz. Katja comes out of the bathroom, her hair still a little wet. Rick nudges her and then points to Franz. Katja just looks at him for a moment. Then she approvingly looks at Rick and nods. Katja walks out to Franz and hugs him.

She leans towards Franz's ear and whispers, "thank you for being there."

Then she gives him a grateful peck on the cheek.

Franz simply nods. Then he looks at her and asks, "are you and Rick, okay?"

"We have to be," Katja says sternly.

Franz understood.

Rick joins them on the balcony.

"I think it is time we have a big talk," he says. Franz agrees.

Katja then goes downstairs to find Sabine. She is in the basement, and the kids are watching *The Pirates of the Caribbean*. Sabine gets up and hugs Katja and they walk upstairs together.

Katja looks at Sabine.

"Sabine, I am starving. I think it is time for us to have a big family dinner tonight."

Sabine looks at her a little concerned.

"That may take some time," she says.

"No, it can be just bread and sliced meats like we eat on flat plates," Katja says. "Just a quick dinner, but all of us need to sit down and talk a second. All good family things start at the dinner table. Oh, and that includes Franz."

Sabine hugs Katja again and nods her head.

"I got this. Give me about five minutes."

Katja returns to Franz and Rick upstairs.

"Franz, we need to sit down and eat. I want you to eat with us as well," she says.

Franz looks puzzled for a moment.

"Give me a moment," he says. "I am going to get someone here while we eat."

Katja smiles as Franz makes a phone call.

Katja grabs Rick's arm and says, "let's go help Sabine a moment."

Rick and Sabine walk downstairs. A few minutes later, the doorbell rings. Sabine answers the door and smiles. A big man, about 6 foot 5 and probably weighing a good 250 pounds, smiles back.

"Wilkommen, Ralf!" Sabine says.

"Oh Danke, my lovely Sabine," Ralf responds.

Sabine guides him in and takes him to Franz. Rick looks at him as they pass by and has a puzzled look on his face.

"Rick, this is Ralf," Sabine says, noticing his look of confusion. "He will stay the night on the balcony."

"Thank you, Ralf," Rick responds.

"No problem," Ralf smiles.

Franz comes downstairs while Sabine brings all the kids upstairs. They all meet in the kitchen, and everyone sits down. Franz sits next to Sebastian and Emma at the table.

Katja looks around and says, "let's pray."

Everyone grabs their neighbor's hands. Franz smiles as Emma and Sebastian hold his hands.

"Dear Lord," Katja prays. "Thank you for our wonderful family. May you watch over each of us here tonight, for everyone at this table is family to us and please watch over Ben. Thank you again, Lord, for watching over us today, amen."

Before anyone starts eating, Katja announces why they are all here.

"Okay, guys, we are going to eat. I need to get a bite down really quick. Then I am going to talk to you about something."

Jonas grabs a piece of Brötchen. "Are you going to talk to us about Emma kissing Randy?" he says.

"What?" Katja exclaims.

Everyone starts to laugh or giggle. Emma is red and looking right through Jonas.

"Twins are not supposed to act this way, but you two do," Rick says, shaking his head.

Katja quickly puts together some Brötchen with butter and a slice of Schinken and cheese and takes a bite.

"Oh my gosh, this is so good," she moans.

The boys look at her puzzled.

"Mom, are you okay?" Noah asks.

"Oh yes, mein Schatz, I am fine," Katja replies with a reassuring smile.

Katja takes her last bite of her Brötchen, drinks coke, and says, "Okay, everyone, I want you to listen up while you eat. No shenanigans, this is serious."

All the kids, Franz, Sabine and Rick turn to look at her.

Katja decides to start from the very beginning.

"So," Katja starts. "When we got to Germany that first night, Dad and I were offered a second job. We were offered to..." she pauses for a moment, then continues. "To be spies. Franz met us and offered that if we were to be spies for our country, you guys would always be taken care of, along with Uncle Ben."

Jonas looks at Katja.

"Like James Bond?" he asks.

"More like Jason Bourne than Bond," Rick proudly responds.

Noah has an exciting, shocking look and says, "cool."

Sebastian looks at Rick and smiles.

"Seriously, we have been keeping this from you since the night we got here," Katja says. "Sabine is your nanny, but she is also here to protect you. She is our family. Franz coordinates things for us. I want you to know that he is here for us. He is family. I need you to understand that."

Katja looks around the room and sees that everyone is still focused on her. She continues.

"In our minds, you have the best protection in the world. But we have a problem, and that's why we are talking."

Now, Rick starts in.

"Even though Sabine will protect you, there are times you are not here, and if you don't know what we do, someone could take advantage of your innocence," he says. "But, if you do know, then you know what to look for and how to beware of bad people."

"Are there a lot of bad people?" Sebastian asks.

"Most people are not bad," Katja says. "But because of what we do, there are people who will try almost anything to get at Mom or Dad, including going after you. We want to prepare you. So, you won't have to worry, but instead, you are just careful about what you do. Does that make sense?"

Sebastian nods, and so do the rest of the kids.

"I want to make this clear, this can never be told to anyone," Rick says seriously. "This is the family secret. Only the people in this room know this secret, and we have to keep it that way. Do we understand?" Everyone nods in agreement and Rick continues.

"Now, this is just as important; nothing comes before our family. Nothing," he says. "We guard our secrets and each other. It is us at this table and Uncle Ben. After the family, everything else is secondary."

Everyone nods and Noah asks, "is Uncle Ben safe?"

"Well, first, your Uncle Ben is safe," Franz says. "He was moved to a new facility in Texas. It is considered one of the best. Next, I would like to say; I am glad to be part of the family. Your Mom and Dad are wonderful people, and they are doing great things. I have known Sabine for some time, and she is the right fit for the family. To be honest, we will be in each other's lives until I pass away."

"We are so close that Sabine even saw your dad naked tonight," Katja says jokingly. The kids giggle while Rick looks around and whistles nonchalantly.

"Ew," Emma says while making a face.

"We *are* family, we saw Sabine naked," Noah blurts out.

Everyone at the table laughs. Sabine shakes her head and laughs.

"What, young man?" Katja exclaims.

"Yep, we saw her boobies and her mushi," Noah continues on.

"Who is this we?" Rick asks.

Noah wastes no time telling.

"Oh, Michael, Jonas, and me," he says with a big smile. "We were watching her in the shower through the window and she came out completely naked. Dad, she came out of the bathroom naked and made us look in her eyes and not her body."

"It seems you learned a lot of lessons that day," Rick says. "You got to see a naked woman, and you learned that the most important part is her eyes."

"But it was more fun looking at her body than her eyes," Jonas laughs.

Sabine just shakes her head and rolls her eyes. Everyone at the table laughs harder.

"Mom, we knew something was up because you and Dad were leaving more. Working out more," Michael says. "Suddenly you are here, and suddenly Sabine is taking us to the movies. We are all doing martial arts and breaking boards in the front yard. There were clues, Dad. We're not dumb."

Rick looks at him and says, "we know that son, and that is why we wanted to have this talk."

Franz looks at Rick and asks, "if I may?"

Rick laughs. "Franz, you are part of the family. We have heard everything else tonight."

"Katja and Rick, you are not alone on this," Franz says. "Most families in the Agency are faced with this. Surprisingly the majority are doing the same thing that you are doing tonight. We have found it quelled fears and puts the family in a safer position, but it is always the family's decision."

Rick nods and then turns to Sabine.

"Sabine, if you don't mind, I think Franz, Katja, and I have to discuss tonight's events," he says. She smiles.

"Don't worry, Rick, I got them."

Rick, Franz and Katja all walk upstairs to the balcony and Katja takes a Brötchen sandwich with her.

Rick looks at her and says, "Hungry, are we?"

Katja smiles, takes a bite while growling, and says with food in her mouth, "I was starving, my love."

Ralf stands by steady as can be, looking out over the road by the front yard.

"Ralf will be here tonight. He won't leave," Franz assures.

"Thanks, Ralf," Rick says.

"No problem," Ralf replies. "Y'all sleep easy tonight."

Franz then looks at Rick and Katja.

"So, what did we find?" he asks.

"We got some good photos of Lena's place," Rick replies. "We are pretty sure the mixer is an American from Harvey Barracks. They also seem frustrated with the mixer. Either the mixer is new or isn't reliable. There was a page with names on it and sickles by certain names. We also have some dates and names of the targets. They want revenge for the RAF killings, from what I could tell. One page had, 'make them pay' written on it. Their target seems to be any German that had any dealings with killing of the RAF, but also Gerhard Schröder and George W. Bush." Rick looks at Franz and says, "further down that same page, they say, 'embarrass Germany by killing the American President on German soil. Sever the alliance.' I guess Schröder is stopping in Würzburg for a speaking engagement with President Bush on October 15th. That is the date."

Franz checks the date on his watch.

"That is not far away. We will have to end this quickly then," he says.

Katja continues. "In Lena's apartment, we also found some photos of Lena and maybe Andreas naked but that was about it there."

"Guys, that was a gold mine," Franz says. "Now we have the target and date. We can work with that. We will need to conduct more terminations in the Sharp Sickle to eradicate them hopefully."

Rick and Katja smile at the praise.

Franz then says, "let's talk about Otto and his apartment."

"Oh, before we do," Rick says. "We got a photo of Lena's password, the computer, and computer type. There is a list from the sheet from the computer."

Franz smiles. "You two are getting good at this," he says.

"Thanks, but Otto's apartment was insane," Katja says. "In there, we found some photos of several members of the Sharp Sickle. There are a bunch of photos of the members showing off their sickle tattoos and topless, both men and women. The Honey Girl has her sickle tattoo below one of her tits. Some photos show their faces, mainly the ones with the tattoo on the neck, and some have their faces blacked out. It seems they are trying to keep them hidden. Then Rick found a photo by Otto's computer of Sebastian riding a bike and a second one of Emma on a moped. That's what led to tonight's conversation."

"If he has that, then one of the others could too," Franz says.

"They had a photo of Hermann kissing me and me grabbing his crotch outside the Airport Club," Katja goes on. "And on the top, it had handwritten on it, 'Schwarze Witwe, Zauberin, Frau des Todes, Verührerin.' Otto had other photos regarding the Airport Club and me. While we were fighting, he asked if I fucked Hermann or if I was a tease. Otto kept referring to me as a little seductress. He also said he took the photos."

"So, he may just have the photos and no one else, or they all have them. We don't really know." Franz says.

Rick nods in agreement.

"I don't think we can take the chance of taking the easy way on this," he says.

Franz agrees.

"Nope, I say, let me kill them all," Katja says harshly.

"So, what happened inside when Otto returned?" Franz asks.

"Well," Katja says. "I was coming out of the bathroom, and I saw him for a second. He lunged at Rick, and I tried to yell out, but it was too late. He hit Rick in the back of the head, so I went after Otto, and he grabbed me by the throat and held me up in the air against the wall. I kicked him several times and was able to hit him in his nuts and stomach. He was very strong. He still had me by the throat as we went back and fell on his bed. He ripped my blouse and sports bra completely in two with one swipe. Otto flipped us, and then he was on top. Otto started opening my pants, and I grabbed my dagger and then stabbed him in the neck a few times."

"Do you know how many times you stabbed him?" Franz interrupts.

"Probably about seven or eight times," Katja says. Franz shakes his head and smiles.

"The mop-up guy counted 38 stab wounds on Otto and two gunshot wounds," Franz says.

Katja chuckled for a second "I was pissed," she says. "He had photos of my family, and Rick was down."

"I don't care how many times you stab him as long as you are alive," Franz says. They sit in silence for a moment as Franz looks around.

"Okay, Ralf will be here tonight," he says. "Tomorrow, you go to work. Let me get the cameras so we can look at everything. We will probably step up a few things on this. Right now, we believe Andreas is the leader, and the mixer is an American on Harvey Barracks. We have not ruled out Lieutenant Young on this, either."

"Oh Franz," Rick says. "We start our field exercise Wednesday evening also."

"We will figure out how to get you back on that," Franz says. "Let's talk Tuesday evening."

"Sounds good," Katja says with a yawn. "I am going to bed. I am exhausted." Rick agrees and Franz leaves the house. Rick looks in the kitchen, and sees Sabine is there.

"Sabine is everything good?" Rick asks.

Sabine smiles. "Yes, it is Rick. It was a good dinner tonight. Are you and Katja okay?"

"Yeah, I think we are," Rick nods.

"Good go gets some rest," Sabine says.

Rick smiles and works his way upstairs and checks on the kids along the way up. They are all asleep. Rick can see Ralf, still outside on the balcony, steady as can be. Rick then makes his way to the top floor and to his room. He walks in and finds Katja passed out on the bed, still with clothes on. He slides the blanket out from underneath her then slowly pulls her pants off. He then puts the blanket over her, and he crawls into bed to go to sleep. Rick realizes it has been a long day, and some of it he doesn't remember. He looks at Katja and just feels grateful that she is his wife.

REPORT FROM
LIEUTENANT TRAVIS

*M*onday morning PT formation, Katja is there tired and still feeling exhausted. She sees Lieutenant Travis is all smiles, so Katja knows her date went well for her. Katja also notices Lieutenant Young there.

"Staff Sergeant Taylor, I saw your husband this weekend at Globus," Lieutenant Young says as she walks up to Katja.

Katja smiles. "Oh really?"

"Yeah," Lieutenant Young says. "I have some friends of my dad that live over here, and I told them I would help them out refurbishing some things while I am here. I promised my Dad to look in on them. They would come and visit us in America quite a bit."

"That's cool," Katja says.

"I learned German from them at an early age, and they would let me come over in the summers and stay with them," Lieutenant Young says.

Katja smiles, and as she does, Lieutenant Travis comes over as well.

"Staff Sergeant Taylor, after PT, I've got to tell you about my weekend."

Katja smiles. "It seems it went well for you," she says.

Lieutenant Travis nods enthusiastically.

PT starts with the company doing some Calisthenics. Katja is doing them, too, but her mind is racing, thinking about Lieutenant Young's words. She believes the reasoning makes sense for everything with her, but who could it be if that is the case? And the mixer is supposedly in Harvey Barracks? There are other Battalions on the base where she doesn't know a single person. This could change everything. They may be back to square one with the mixer, and the target date is only a few weeks away. As she is doing some side-straddle hops, she sees Rick out the corner of her eye. She is grateful for that man. Her mind thinks back to Otto's house and the big fight. Katja cannot believe she stabbed him 38 times. She is trying to recant each blow and stab that happened. She refocuses back on the side-straddle hops and finds herself soaked in sweat. Katja laughs at it and thinks it's better to focus on PT, not killing someone. Her reflections had her heartrate going up.

After PT, she is too tired to go home so she takes a shower at the gym instead. While at the gym shower, she sees Lieutenant Travis there. Since the shower is a common shower with about 18 water picks in there, Lieutenant Travis and Katja go in together.

Lieutenant Travis smiles.

"Staff Sergeant Taylor, I had a wonderful time with John this weekend," she tells her excitedly.

"Is John, Lieutenant Piper?" Katja asks.

Lieutenant Travis smiles and says, "yes."

Katja notices that Lieutenant Travis has some hickies on her neck, by her breasts, and one on her inner thigh. Katja looks around at the other women showering with them and no one is paying attention. She walks up close to Lieutenant Travis.

"These are okay," Katja says as she points and touches the hickies on her breasts and her thigh. Then she touches the one on her neck. "Ma'am, that one will get you in trouble in the Army. Make sure you wear your T-shirt backward to help cover it up and also keep your collar high."

Lieutenant Travis initially feels awkward but realizes what Katja was doing.

"Thank you," she says in a low voice.

Then Katja smiles. "From the look of things, it seems like you had an excellent weekend."

A glow illuminates Lieutenant Travis but her expression quickly changes.

"Did you get in a fight with Sergeant First Class Taylor this weekend?" she asks, concerned.

"Ma'am? What do you mean?" Katja responds in a questioning tone.

"You have some bruises or rug burns," Lieutenant Travis says, then she pauses and says, "Oh, on your back."

Katja realizes that her marks were from being slammed up against the wall by Otto. "Yeah, my man is a beast," she lies as she winks at Lieutenant Travis. "It seems your man is too."

Lieutenant Travis blushes.

"He is a lot of fun," she says.

Katja looks at Lieutenant Travis as they start to get out of the shower and dry off.

"So, tell me about your weekend with John."

"Well," Lieutenant Travis excitedly says, then she looks around to see if anyone is close by, and she whispers, "Katja, we didn't get out of bed all day Saturday. Oh, it was so great! He is such a great man. He made me breakfast in bed. We took our time and just enjoyed each other."

Katja looks at her and asks, "Ma'am, have you ever had a boyfriend before?"

"No, not really," Lieutenant Travis says.

"Ma'am, are you on birth control?" Katja asks.

"I have been meaning to talk to you about that," Lieutenant Travis says.

"Okay," Katja says. "Today, let's schedule an appointment and get you taken care of. We don't need little Lieutenant Travis and Lieutenant Pipers running around yet."

"Yeah, my parents would so kill me," Lieutenant Travis laughs.

Katja laughs, then says, "Ma'am, listen to me on this. This guy really seems great but don't go all-in just yet. You can have fun; you can have crazy sex and fuck each other till you pass out and all." Then Katja taps her on the forehead and says, "but don't go all in up here; give that some time. You have only known him for a little while, so don't make life decisions just yet. You are an adult now. Everyone fucks, so don't think that it doesn't happen with everyone just because he does it with you. I am being blunt on this, so you see it."

Lieutenant Travis understands and nods in agreement.

Katja looks at Lieutenant Travis. "Do you want to get breakfast?" she asks.

Lieutenant Travis smiles.

"Yes. Do you know a good place?"

Katja smiles. "We are going to eat in the chow hall. Have you eaten there yet?"

Lieutenant Travis shakes her head. "No, not much."

"Soldiers need to see you eat in there," Katja says. "In fact, if you see your soldiers in there, you eat with them. You find out everything you want to know about your troops at the table. Sometimes things you don't want to know. But the soldiers respect and trust you more if you break bread with them."

"I'm all in," Lieutenant Travis says.

Katja and Lieutenant Travis grab their tray at the chow hall, and they see two soldiers from their platoon. Katja approaches them.

"Private Jones, you don't mind if I sit here, do you?" she asks.

"No, not at all Staff Sergeant," Private Jones says.

"The Ma'am will eat with us too," Katja says as they sit down at the table. "How are you doing, Specialist Caine?"

"Oh, I am doing fine, Staff Sergeant," Specialist Caine responds. Katja looks at Caine.

"Specialist, why don't you tell the Lieutenant what you do in the platoon, where you live, and where you are from?" she suggests.

"Too easy, Staff Sergeant," Specialist Caine says. Katja points to the Lieutenant so Specialist Caine will address her. "Ma'am, I work on trucks in the 3rd shop. I am from Louisiana. I used to live in the barracks, but I married a German girl, so now I live in Rodelsee."

"How long have you been married?" Lieutenant Travis asks.

"Oh, we have been married about six months," Specialist Caine replies. "We are expecting a baby in the next few weeks."

There is a silence around the table, and then Katja speaks up.

"Specialist Caine, does your wife work?"

"Staff Sergeant!" Specialist Caine replies. Katja waves him off and points to the Ma'am. "Ma'am," Specialist Caine says. "No, she does not work."

"Are you prepared for this baby?" Katja asks.

"I am not sure about that," Specialist Caine says. "It moved really fast."

"Will your wife follow you on the next assignment, or will she want to stay in Germany?" Katja then asks Specialist Caine. Specialist Caine thinks for a moment.

"Ma'am and Staff Sergeant, no, she wants to come to America. We love each other," he says.

"Good, I am glad to hear that Specialist Caine," Katja replies. "It sounds like you have a really good woman." Specialist Caine smiles, and then Katja asks, "Will you have enough money to pay your bills?"

"I barely have enough money as it is," Specialist Caine says.

"Come see me and the Lieutenant today," Katja says. "We will sit down with you on your bills and get you over to some financial counseling. It is a good thing, okay?"

"Yes, Staff Sergeant and Ma'am," Specialist Caine smiles.

Katja turns to Private Jones. "So Private Jones, the Lieutenant has some questions for you."

"Do you live in the barracks?" Lieutenant Travis asks. "And please tell me why you came to the Army."

"Ma'am, I live on the second floor of the barracks," Private Jones says. "My brother was in the army, and he told me to get out of our hometown or I'll eventually be in trouble. He said the Army was a way for me to escape."

"Are your parents proud of you?" Lieutenant Travis asks.

Private Jones smiles. "Yes, Ma'am, they sure are. My Mom takes my picture to church every Sunday and shows everyone."

"Where is home?" Lieutenant Travis asks.

"Memphis, Ma'am," Private Jones says.

They take a moment for everyone to finish eating their breakfast.

"Hey guys," Katja says as she and Lieutenant Travis stand up. "The Ma'am and I got to get. Thanks for sharing breakfast with us."

Katja and Lieutenant Travis leave the chow hall after returning their trays. Lieutenant Travis looks at Katja.

"Wow, you are so natural at this. I see what you mean. In those 20 minutes, I learned more about my soldiers than I have in the last three months," she says. Katja looks at her.

"Ma'am, you did great," she says. "Remember, it has to be sincere and genuine, and they will follow you anywhere. If you don't believe me, I will tell you right now Specialist Caine, and Private Jones are telling their buddies what a great officer you are. Remember, a soldier craves attention, especially from officers."

LIEUTENANT MOORE RETURNS

Rick arrives at work on Tuesday morning. He is looking forward to Lieutenant Moore's return. The Field Exercise starts tomorrow, and it will be demanding on everyone. He needs his Lieutenant back and in the game. Rick walks to his office, and he sees Lieutenant Moore and Lieutenant Sawyer having a loud argument that can be heard down the hall. Rick knocks on the door and walks in.

"Gentlemen," he says. "Officers shouldn't be heard down the hall. That is normally left for Sergeants."

Lieutenant Moore understood, and Lieutenant Sawyer storms off. Rick looks at Lieutenant Moore.

"Sounds like you guys had a great time in Garmisch."

"Sergeant First Class Taylor," Lieutenant Moore says. "I wanted to kill him. That is the dumbest SOB I have ever met."

"Really?" Rick responds. "So, what happened?"

"Let's lock the door," Lieutenant Moore says. "I don't want anyone coming in as I talk about this."

Rick locks the door. Lieutenant Moore then explains.

"We get down there late Thursday evening," he starts. "Once at Garmisch, we have a few drinks, and everything is fine. We agreed to link up for breakfast on Friday, and we were going to the Zugspitze for the day. The next morning, Karen comes down to the breakfast table in tears. She had been balling all night. They got in a fight, and he left after midnight. He didn't come back until early Monday morning. Julie went to Karen's room and spent the whole weekend with her. We never left the hotel area the whole weekend. Here we are in one of the most beautiful places on earth, and we stay inside the hotel the whole time. Monday morning, he comes back, all smiles like nothing happened."

"Where did he go?" Rick asks.

"No one knows," Lieutenant Moore says. "He wouldn't tell anyone. I feel bad for Karen because she is just destroyed and embarrassed."

"I can imagine," Rick responds. Lieutenant Moore looks at Rick.

"Just now, when you came up, I told him I would never go to a non-army event with him again. He told me I was taking it too far. I spent $800 on our hotel this weekend just to sit there. Sergeant First Class Taylor, this dude is a lost cause."

Rick just shakes his head. Then Rick says, "Hey Sir, we got this field exercise tomorrow. So, we got to get back in the ballgame here."

"Yeah, I know," Lieutenant Moore says. "Don't worry, I am all in."

"Good," Rick replies. "Sir, I left some information about the mission and unit on your desk. I've got to check on our vehicles. I will be back later."

Rick walks the motor pool; Lieutenant Sawyer comes running up to him.

Rick salutes him and says, "good morning, Sir."

Why is this guy wanting to talk to me? Rick thinks. Lieutenant Sawyer salutes back and says, "Hey, Sergeant First Class Taylor, how was your weekend?"

"It was good, Sir," Rick replies.

"Did you do anything cool this weekend?" Lieutenant Sawyer asks.

"Not really, Sir," Rick answers.

"So, what kind of beer do you like to drink?" Lieutenant Sawyer asks.

"Often the free kind, but if I am buying it's either a Shiner Bock from America or a Radler here in Germany," Rick replies. "What about you, Sir?"

Lieutenant Sawyer smiles. "Oh, I like a Dunkel. You know the dark stuff," he says, "I hear you got a lot of kids."

Before Rick could answer, Katja walks up and salutes Lieutenant Sawyer, who swiftly salutes back.

"Sir," Katja says, "Do you mind if I have a moment with Sergeant First Class Taylor?"

"Oh, no problem," Lieutenant Sawyer says.

Rick looks at her as they start walking toward her office. He leans over and whispers, "thank you. You just saved me."

"What do you mean?" Katja asks.

"Well, first of all, he left Lieutenant Moore and them while they were down in Garmisch," Rick replies. "I guess he got in a fight with his wife, and he left late Thursday night and didn't show back up until Monday morning."

"What a fucking douche," Katja replies.

"Now, he is like trying to be my friend or something. What a weird fucker," Rick says.

Katja shakes her head then looks at Rick.

"Oh, my goodness, Lieutenant Travis is too pure for the army." Katja laughs. "She is new to men and sex. She is new on dealing with troops and so on, but she is honest and true, which is a good thing. I can work with her. She is moldable." Katja smiles.

"She sounds 1000 times better than Lieutenant Sawyer," Rick says. Katja agrees.

"Oh," Katja suddenly says. "Let me tell you about Lieutenant Young from yesterday. Apparently, she has some family friends that she used to come here and visit. I don't know if her story is true or if it is a diversion. But if it is true, then she is not the mixer."

Rick looks at her. "What do you believe?" he asks.

Katja, without hesitation, says, "it's not her."

"Katja you are never wrong with your gut feeling. You have a great knack for that," Rick replies. "Well, we see Franz tonight. We need to tell him."

Katja nods in agreement and then smiles. "Oh, another thing from yesterday," she says. "Tonight, I can tell you stories of all the women in the showers soaping up their boobies and washing each other off."

Rick smiles. "Just what I need before we go to the field," he says as Katja laughs.

"Hey, I got to get back in here with Lieutenant Moore to get him ready," Rick says.

"Sounds good, my lover," Katja replies in a sexy voice.

Rick smiles and walks away.

Katja looks around as Rick walks away. She then looks at her watch to check the time.

"Staff Sergeant Taylor," Someone calls out.

Katja looks up, and it's Lieutenant Sawyer. *Oh no, I can't stand this dude,* Katja thinks to herself as Lieutenant Sawyer walks over. "How are you, Staff Sergeant Taylor?" he says in a sarcastic tone.

"Oh, I am good, Sir," Katja replies.

"You know my wife, Karen," he says. "She loves to cook Schnitzel. What do you like to cook?"

Katja looks at him, almost repulsed, takes a step towards him.

"Are you hitting on me, Sir?" she asks. "You know my husband would kill you if he thought that." Katja looks him up and down in disgust. "By the way, regards to cooking and eating understand this; I eat my meat raw. I am the apex predator," she says with a slight growl in her voice. She then turns and walks away.

"How did we let *that*, in the army?" Katja mumbles to herself as she walks away.

FRANZ AND PLANS

*F*ranz stops by the Taylor's house on Adalbert-Stifter Strasse. It is about 7 p.m., and Sabine answers the door.

Sabine smiles when she sees who it is.

"Come on in, Franz," she says.

Franz returns the smile. "Thank you, Sabine."

Once inside, Emma walks by and says hi to Franz. Franz smiles and returns the hello.

"Rick and Katja are downstairs in the basement," Sabine tells him.

Franz nods his head and says, "How has Ralf been?"

"Fine," Sabine says. "He has only left that place to use the restroom and eat."

"Good," Franz smiles.

Franz heads downstairs. Once there, he knocks on the basement door, and finds Rick and Katja inside.

Rick turns around and waves to Franz.

"Hi, how are you doing, Franz?" he asks.

Franz smiles. "Good, my friend," he replies. "I see you two are ready to go play soldier for a few weeks."

Katja looks at Franz with a dreaded look. "Yes, we are."

"Okay, tell me where you two will be at for the first week," Franz says.

"On the first day, I will be in Grafenwöhr, return Thursday afternoon, and then be in Klosterforst for the weekend," Rick replies. "The first few days of next week, I will be in the rear as well."

Katja jumps in now. "I will be in the rear for the first week," she says. "I head to Grafenwöhr for a few days and then back to the rear the second week. We don't have any operations in Klosterforst."

"You know we have had spies and issues here since the 60s," Franz says. "In the early 80s, foreign spies flocked to Klosterforst to see the first M1 Abrams train against the Canadian forces in Operation Carbine Fortress. This area of Germany is where the M1 got the nickname Whispering Death because the Canadians never heard them until they were killed off in the training battles. So, we have had our share of espionage around here, and times haven't changed."

"Wow, I didn't know that" Rick replies.

"So, let's get into the game plan of things, to drive a stake in the Sharp Sickles heart. Friday evening, Rick and Katja, both of you will need to be here by 8 p.m."

"That won't be a problem," Katja says.

Rick looks and says, "I shouldn't have a problem either. I will be in Klosterforst."

"Good," Franz replies. "There will be a pizza box for you when you arrive here from Arvino's. Take that with you. Then at 8:10, you two need to head over to Lena's place. She gets out of work at 8:30 pm, and so far, she goes straight home. When she arrives, terminate her. Directly after that, go to Andreas' place and use the pizza box as a delivery. Once he opens the door, make your way into his place. He will not expect pizza, but Katja, tell him you were told this is the address, be persistent, distracting, but get in. Rick can be down the hall. No matter what, get in the room. Terminate him as well. Find what information you can and get out. We believe he is the head of the snake and if we take him out, that will be the end of this, we hope."

"Oh Franz, I don't think Lieutenant Young is the mixer," Katja says. "I got her story, and it is pretty plausible from the sound of it. She has family friends over here, and she has been refurbishing."

"We will check it out," Franz says. "But if that is the case and the mixer is an American from Harvey Barracks, we are back to square one on this. That is disappointing."

"I agree," Rick says.

"What about the Honey Girl?" Katja asks.

"We stick to these two here," Franz says. "Not sure we would have time without someone missing you too much."

Katja looks at Rick. "I see your girlfriend gets a free pass," she says bitterly.

Rick just shakes his head.

"How long is Ralf staying here?" Rick asks.

"As long as you would like," Franz says.

"I think we are good for right now," Rick replies.

"If we need him back, Sabine has his number as well," Franz replies. "I assure you he will be here within ten minutes."

Katja smiles. "Thank you, Franz."

Franz walks towards the door but stops short. "Oh, I forgot," he says. "Here are your cameras back also. Great information. You may need them tonight as well."

Franz hands the cameras back to Rick and Katja.

"Well, I will go now, you two have fun in the field, and I will see you two sometime Friday."

"Sounds good, Franz," Rick replies.

LENA AND ANDREAS

R ick is in Klosterforst doing field exercise and looks at Lieutenant Moore.

"Sir, I will need to go to the rear for about two or three hours. I got to check on some troops and pick up a few things for the ones out here," Rick informs him.

"No problem, Sergeant First Class Taylor, take your time," Lieutenant Moore says.

Rick heads out of Klosterforst in his Hummer to the company headquarters. It is about a 15 min drive in a military vehicle. Once he arrives there, he heads home. It is Friday, and he will be on his big mission in a short time.

Katja is in her car pulling out the gate of the post. She is ready to get home and get going on the mission. She is not happy about the Honey Girl not being on the mission list, but she *is* excited about the other two on the mission.

Rick arrives home first. Sabine greets him at the door.

"You two be safe tonight," she says.

"We will," Rick replies. "Hopefully, we will be back soon."

"Oh," Sabine says suddenly. "Your pizza is in the oven, just to stay safe and warm. It's still in the box."

Rick smiles. "Awesome," he says then he goes upstairs. A few minutes later, Katja walks through the door and greets Sabine.

Sabine smiles. "Hey Katja," she says. "I showed Rick where the pizza is for your mission. You two be safe. Okay?"

"We will," Katja says before she runs upstairs to change clothes.

Rick and Katja are both wearing comfortable jeans. Rick has a T-shirt with a shoulder harness holding his Beretta and a sports jacket over it. Katja is wearing similar attire, but her shirt is green. She has her dagger in the same place along her belt. They are both wearing sneakers for maneuverability.

Katja and Rick get in the car and look at each other.

"Katja, you ready?" Rick says.

"Yes, my love," she replies. "Let's do this."

They arrive at Lena's place at exactly 8:10 pm and move to her apartment. Once again, Rick picks the lock, and they walk in. The apartment looks exactly the same as it did the last time they were there.

"Let's either hang out in the bedroom or one of us behind the door and the other in the living room. Which do you prefer?" Rick asks.

Katja looks around the room.

"I prefer the bedroom," she says with a smile as she lifts her eyebrows and her head simultaneously a couple of times at Rick. "Rick, you know that's what I prefer."

Rick smiles and shakes his head before he finally replies.

"Okay, you sit on the bed and wait for her to come through the door," he says. "She won't be able to see you until she gets in. I will be in the bathroom. Once she gets in the bedroom, I will step behind her to prevent her from leaving."

"Sounds good," Katja says.

Rick checks the time on his watch and sees that it is 8:40. He walks into the bathroom while Katja sits on the bed with her back to the headboard. From this angle, she can see when the door opens and if anyone enters.

The front door tumbler clicks and both Katja and Rick can hear the door open. Footsteps move through the house, and they hear the second door open. The sound of keys hitting the counter can be heard, then someone proceeds to the bedroom. The bedroom door opens, and Lena walks in with her head down. Her pink hair is highly visible even in the dim lighting. Lena is wearing blue nursing tops and bottoms. She doesn't notice Katja as she heads to the bathroom. As the bedroom door shuts behind her, Katja stands up and puts her hand on the door to ensure it.

"Well, good evening there, Lena," Katja says.

Startled, Lena jumps for a second and turns around. A visible shock floods her face.

"I know who you are," Lena says. "You are the girl that was with Hermann before he disappeared."

"Really, are we still on that?" Katja replies. "A girl gets a damn bad reputation for being seen with one guy for one lousy night, and she never hears the end of it. You see how this works." Katja shakes her head sideways. Rick slowly walks behind Lena who isn't aware of his presence. Rick then says, "do you know who I am?"

Lena, surprised to hear another voice, turns around and looks at Rick.

"No, who are you?" she asks.

"Good," Rick replies. "And we will keep it that way."

With Lena effectively surrounded, Katja begins interrogating her.

"So, what's the deal with the neck tattoo?" Katja asks. "It seems you like sickles."

Lena looks Katja over. "What's not to love about them?" Lena asks. "We are rising, and we will be strong again."

"So does your mixer have one of those also?" Katja asks.

"We all have them," Lena replies. "Just some of us don't have them on our necks, and some are in more fun places."

"So, who is the mixer?" Katja asks.

"Oh, you will be surprised," Lena smiles. "Soon, you will see."

Rick pushes Lena forwards a bit, and he leans his back to the door.

"So, what you're saying is you're not going to tell us who the mixer is?" Katja asks.

Lena smiles. "Nope."

Katja pulls out her gun and points it at Lena. Lena freezes in place, then she looks Katja in the eyes and lifts her head, calling her bluff. Katja emotionlessly shoots her in the left leg. Lena screams and falls to the floor.

Blood is flowing out of Lena's wound. Smoke is slowly rising out of the suppressor. Lena is quivering in pain, her whole-body trembling. Her chin shudders as she looks up at Katja. The shell casing can be heard spinning on the floor.

"You're a nurse," Katja says. "You can bandage that if you answer my question. I will ask you one more time, who is the mixer?" Katja raises her gun to Lena's forehead.

Lena pushes her chest out, shaking. "I would rather die than-"

Another gunshot goes off before she finishes her sentence. The air fills with the smell of burning gunpowder; smoke billows out of Katja's Beretta. The second shell casing is spinning on the floor.

Katja looks at Rick. "I am not begging that bitch. Either she talks and dies, or she just dies," she says. "I didn't need to hear all that gibberish, that 'I am tough to the last-second' bullshit. She wasn't going to tell us what we wanted to hear, and I wasn't going to listen to what she wanted to say."

Rick smirks. "Totally with you, my love."

Rick takes out his phone and sends Franz a note.

We need a mop-up at Lena's. All is good on our end. Also, have a crew take the computer and the sheet under the keyboard.

Rick looks under the keyboard and notices the list with the sickles by their name. The mixer is on there, and next to the word mixer is "JS" and then a sickle. Rick can't figure it out. He takes a photo of it.

Katja looks at Rick and says, "okay time to get, my love."

"Yes, it is," Rick replies.

Rick and Katja get in their car and ride down the street to Andreas's place. They park down the road about 100 yards away. Rick goes in first, and Katja waits about two minutes before she proceeds to the building with the pizza box. Rick walks past the apartment door and leans against the wall out of sight of the door opens. Katja arrives at the door, looks over at Rick, about four feet away, and gives him a wink. She is holding the pizza with her left hand and rings the doorbell with her right. She hears movement in the apartment, and Andreas opens the door and looks at her in confusion.

"Hi, I am here to deliver a pizza, a pepperoni pizza," Katja replies.

"There is a mistake," Andreas says. "I didn't order a pizza."

"The address says-" Katja begins to say, then Rick jumps out, pushes the door into Andreas and shoves his way into the apartment before Katja could finish her sentence. Andreas falls to the ground. Rick pulls out his gun and points it at Andreas. Katja walks in, throws the pizza on the floor, and kicks the door shut.

Katja smiles and looks directly at Andreas.

"Who doesn't like pepperoni pizza? Andreas!" she says.

Andreas looks at Katja and suddenly recognizes her.

"You're the one with Hermann, the seductress," he says as fear visibly engulfs his face.

Katja looks at Rick annoyed and rolls her eyes.

"Really, again?" she says. "One wrong man in my lifetime and I am to be judged by that?" Katja looks over at Andreas, shakes her head in anger and says, "Get your damn ass on the couch."

Rick keeps his gun on Andreas while he moves to the couch.

"Lock the door," Rick instructs Katja.

Katja moves to lock the door.

"Pull your gun out and check the rest of the apartment," Rick tells her.

Katja does precisely that. She walks into his kitchen, then into his bedroom. She pulls open the Schrank doors in the bedroom and checks under the bed. Katja then moves to the bathroom. In there, she pulls back the shower curtain.

"All clear," She reports as she returns to the living room where Rick and Andreas are.

Katja looks at Rick.

"Maybe we should do the questioning in the bedroom?" she says while rolling her eyes. Then she looks at Andreas, leans her head toward him. "Since everyone thinks I am super easy and all," she says.

She pulls Andreas up by the collar and he cooperates fully. Katja lets go of his collar and moves ahead of him. She walks into the bedroom and turns around to watch Andreas. He walks in with Rick following him. Both Katja and Rick keep their Berettas and eyes on him. Rick tells Andreas to sit on the bed and he takes a seat at the foot of the bed. Katja shuts the bedroom door and stands in front of him while Rick stands behind Andreas and to his right. This way, Katja and Rick don't have each other in their target trajectory.

Andreas is sitting very calmly.

"Since you know who I am," Katja says. "Maybe we can get some answers. But first, who is the man behind you?"

Andreas turns his head and sees the suppressor pointed at his head, and he looks up at Rick, shakes his head, and replies, "no idea."

"What do you know about me?" Katja asks.

"You're the one who was going to fuck or did fuck Hermann before he disappeared," Andreas says. "We call you - how do you say? - a seductress. Some call you an enchantress or even a Black Widow. You are a woman of death."

Katja looks at Rick, shaking her head, and says, "you see how a girl hangs out with one wrong guy for one night, and she gets this type of reputation. I am painted with a big A for adultery on my chest. Might as well tattoo that to my forehead."

Rick smiles as he has his gun on Andreas.

"So, what are you to the Sharp Sickle?" Katja asks. Andreas looks puzzled at first.

"Someone has to give birth to something great," he says with his puffed chest out. "Some pronounced a great organization dead a little premature. I thought a new name would be in order. The Sharp Sickle had to come alive. Especially after what they did to-"

Katja interjects, "yes." She moves quickly closer to him. "To whom? There, Andreas, to who?" She looks up as if to think, then looks back at Andreas, "someone close, maybe?"

Andreas looks at her, realizing she is mocking him.

"Okay, Andreas, just a few more questions, and we can move on. Who is the mixer?" she says.

Andreas smiles. "Oh, soon you will find out," he says.

"Andreas, we are really not in the mood for this 'you will soon find out' bullshit, and it doesn't benefit you well either," Katja says.

"So, answer the question," Rick asks again. "Who is the mixer?"

Andreas just smiles. Katja turns to Rick.

"This mother fucker thinks we are playing," she says.

Rick moves his Beretta from Andreas' head to his knee and squeezes off a round. Andreas screams in pain and falls to the floor. Blood is oozing from his knee as smoke fumes out of Rick's Beretta. The room fills with the scent of burning gunpowder as the casing lands on the blanket of the bed.

Andreas begins to shake from the pain. Katja leans down and looks Andreas in the face, still pointing her gun at him. She sticks the tip of the suppressor to his face to lift his head to face her.

"Hey, fuck face," she says. "Do we look like the type of people who play cutesy games?"

A realization comes over Andreas that he is not going to make it out of there alive. His facial expression changes from calm to that of a man in pain and fearing for his life. Rick reaches over and grabs him by the back of the shirt and pulls him back on the bed. Andreas is holding his leg and knee, steadily shaking and whimpering.

Katja stands up.

"So, you want to tell us who the mixer is?" she asks.

Andreas is breathing heavily now.

"He, he," he says between breaths. "He is an, American, on Harvey Barracks."

"Ja, ja, ja we know that" Katja says.

"That's all I am telling you!" Andreas shouts.

Katja looks at him and says, "you want to know what happened to Hermann?"

Andreas looks surprised. Katja leans back down and looks Andreas seductively in his eyes as she slowly licks her lips.

"Do you want to know if I fucked him or not?" Katja leans closer to his face.

Andreas' eyes get big with shock by Katja's approach. Katja moves her face close to his ear, where he can feel her breath, then looks at Rick. Katja smiles and gives Rick a wink, while she places her left hand on Andreas left knee. She slowly slides her hand over his pants up to his penis. Andreas gasps as she slowly squeezes his penis.

"Andreas, do you want to know if your guy Hermann got inside me?" she asks slowly and sensually. Katja can feel him shake but she can also feel that his manhood is aroused.

I am going to get him excited before we kill him, she thinks. *Oh, this is too easy, it is almost like playing with a toy.* She talks even slower, more seductively, breathing in his ear.

"Andreas," she says, almost moaning with her words. "Do you want to know if Hermann got really deep in me where I would moan, like I am now?"

She pauses a second, still slowly rubbing his penis.

"Andreas!" she moans his name in his ear. "Do you want to know if Hermann fucked me?"

Andreas, shaking uncontrollably in pain lifts his head up and says, "Yes. Yes." Andreas takes a deep breath. "I want to know. I want to know." Saliva comes out of his quivering mouth as he says the words.

Katja moves her head to get face to face with him again then removes her hand from between his legs.

"You said you don't know the man behind you. You might want to ask him," she says with a mischievous grin.

Andreas falls back on the bed in pain and looks at Rick. As he looks at Rick, Katja introduces him.

"That, Andreas, is Hermann's Grim Reaper."

A look of terror comes over Andreas' face as he groans and trembles in pain.

"What?" Andreas gasps. "What happened to Hermann?"

"Well," Rick responds. "I can tell you Hermann didn't fuck anyone." He leans in close to Andreas' face. "Because I shot him in the dick," he finishes. "Oh, he wanted to fuck her badly. But that is hard to do, when you're missing your dick."

Andreas' eyes instantly widen, and he starts shaking even more.

"You can keep your dick if you tell us who the mixer is," Rick offers. "I will only ask you this last time."

Andreas shakes almost uncontrollably. "His name is John," he shouts. "That is all we know. An American named John that works on Harvey Barracks. We have seen and coordinated with him several times."

Rick looks at Katja for a second, then nods his head. Katja nods back.

Rick leans over Andreas with his gun pointing to his head.

"You get to keep your dick, but your Sharp Sickle is going back to the grave," he says. Rick moves his finger to the trigger. "Say hi to your Mama and Papa."

Rick pulls the trigger. The bullet pierces Andreas's forehead, and blood oozes over the bed. Rick looks down at him and says, "yep, he is dead."

Katja pulls out her phone and sends Franz a note.

The second mission needs a mop-up crew. The mission is complete, and we are coming home.

BODY IS MISSING

*D*riving back through Kitzingen to get home, Rick and Katja are wired. The drive is less than eight minutes from Andreas's house.

"Rick, that was actually easier than the first two missions," Katja says.

Rick agrees. "Katja, maybe we are getting good at this," he says. "I will say, I think you are enjoying this almost too much. That was intense."

"Rick, I am having fun with it," Katja replies. "You know I like to push things. I figured if he was going to die, why not die aroused for a moment. I hope that doesn't sound bad."

"Now I understand. For me it was fun," Rick replies.

Katja looks at Rick. "When we get home, I will be there for a couple of hours," she says. "I know you have to get back to work, right?"

"Yep, I do," Rick replies. "It will take me about 30 minutes to get back to Lieutenant Moore once I leave the house."

"I will brief Franz then, so you can get back," Katja says.

"Sounds good, my love," Rick replies.

When they arrive at their house, Rick and Katja walk inside, and Rick runs upstairs. Sabine looks at Katja, turns her head, and gives a thumbs up and then a thumbs down in a questioning way. Katja gives a thumbs up. Sabine smiles and hugs her.

"Sabine, I will hang out here for a few hours, then I will have to go back to work," Katja says.

"The little ones are in bed already, and the other ones will be soon," Sabine replies. "Do you want some wine?"

"I would love some, but better not," Katja says, smiling. "I am officially in the field."

Rick runs back down the stairs dressed in his uniform.

"Got to go, my love, it's already 9:45. I got to get, see you soon." He gets in the car and heads back to work.

Sabine and Katja sit in the living room and start talking about the kids.

"There are a lot of little German girls that really like Jonas and Noah," Sabine says. "Oh, they bat their eyes at them all the time."

Katja smiles. "Well, they are good-looking young men."

"Yes, they are," Sabine replies then says, "Katja, I want to explain what happened with the boys and me in the shower, so you don't think anything bad."

"Oh Sabine, I trust you," Katja replies.

"Do let me explain," Sabine begs. "I was in the shower, and I could hear Noah giggle saying he saw my boobies, so I got out of the shower, opened the bathroom door, and walked out. There were the three boys. They were shocked. I told them to look in my eyes and nowhere else and they each slowly did. I told them that now they had seen me, they didn't need to see me again. They will be looking at girls instead of me. Then as I turned away, I laughed at them and said, 'how funny is it a naked girl stands here in front of you, and you just kept looking in her eyes.' Then I went back to the bathroom."

Katja laughs. "Oh, I bet they were red," she says.

"Yes, they were," Sabine says.

As they continue to laugh, Katja gets a text from Rick.

I'm in the Hummer on my way to Lieutenant Moore.

Katja looks back up at Sabine and smiles. "So, when are you going to do this booty call?"

Sabine laughs. "Probably after everything with the Sharp Sickle is done."

Once again, they are interrupted by a text message, this time from Franz.

We have an issue. The body on the second mission is not there. Be careful.

The doorbell rings and Sabine gets up to answer it. When she opens the door, a man who looks to be an American is standing there.

"Can I help you?" Sabine asks.

"Yes, I am a friend of Rick's," he replies. "He told me to stop by and check on Katja."

Rick arrives out at the field site, and he sees Lieutenant Moore.

"Sir, I am back," Rick says,

"Hey Sergeant First Class Taylor, can you believe this shit?" Lieutenant Moore asks. Rick looks puzzled.

"You don't know?" Lieutenant Moore says.

"I guess not, Sir," Rick replies.

"Well, one each," Lieutenant Moore says. "Always the douchebag, Lieutenant John Sawyer, went on sick call to the rear this morning. The vehicle got there, and he is missing."

"Lieutenant John Sawyer?" Rick repeats.

"That's the one," Lieutenant Moore says.

Rick pulls out his phone and sees a text from Franz.

We have an issue. The body on the second mission is not there. Be careful."

Rick sends a text to Katja immediately.

Look out for Lieutenant Sawyer. JS is John Sawyer.

The man walks in through the door, and Sabine steps toward him.

"Oh, it is okay there, Sabine," the man says.

Katja reads Rick's note and walks to the door where she sees Lieutenant Sawyer standing. Disbelief comes over her face.

"Katja, what is going on?" he says.

The door is still open, and another man walks in along with two women. One of them is the Honey Girl, Gizela Gorski. Sabine looks stunned and her eyes get huge.

Katja says deliberately, "Sabine, go to the top floor with the kids." Sabine moves out.

"Yes," Lieutenant Sawyer says. "Yes, go get the kids."

Gizela walks by Katja and touches her on the lips.

"How is the lip balm doing for you?" Gizela says as she licks her own lips.

Rick looks at Lieutenant Moore and says, "I got to get back. I forgot something."

He runs to the Hummer and races back to post. While driving, he calls Franz.

Franz answers, "Hallo Rick."

"We have a problem," Rick says. "Lieutenant Sawyer is the mixer, his initials are JS, and his first name is John. Lena said it was JS, and Andreas said it was John. He has been missing all day."

"That might account for Andreas' body missing," Franz says.

"Katja is at home, and I am heading that way," Rick says.

"I am too, but I am about twenty minutes out," Franz says.

"I will see you there," Rick replies then hangs up.

Sabine goes to the top floor and checks the gun safes under Rick and Katja's bed. They are both back in place with their Berettas. She pulls out both of them then sees Rick's shoulder harness and puts it on with one Beretta. She then puts a jacket on, takes the suppressor off the other Beretta, and shoves that in the back of her pants. Sabine goes down to the second floor and takes the kids upstairs. Everyone is with her except Michael, who was in his room in the basement. Sabine then calls Michael's phone.

Michael answers. "Yes, Sabine?"

"Michael, listen to me," Sabine says. "There are bad people on the first floor. I have the rest of the kids on the top floor. Michael, do you understand me?"

"Yes Sabine," Michael replies. "Where are Mom and Dad?"

"Katja is on the first floor with the four people. There are two men and two women," Sabine tells him. "You stay in your room and lock the door. Do you understand?"

"I can go help," Michael says.

"No, no, no, listen to me," Sabine says. "Your mom is handling it right now, and she doesn't need to be distracted. Lock your door, get in a corner away and protect yourself."

Michael does as she says, still on the phone. Sabine thinks for a moment and says, "I have a plan, listen carefully. Stay by your phone. I need to make another call."

Sabine calls Franz and fills him in.

"Franz, one of them is very familiar," she says. "He looks like the man that killed my Hans."

"I am on my way, Sabine," Franz replies. "You protect the kids at all costs."

"I will, Franz," Sabine replies.

Downstairs, Lieutenant Sawyer smiles at Katja.

"Oh, the almighty Katja. The best Sergeant in the company. The little seductress herself," he teases. "So, is it ok with Rick that you sleep with other men? Maybe you have time for Pasha or me? Or both of us? Maybe a little officer and enlisted fling along with a civilian? I think you said you eat your meat raw? What would you say?"

Pasha pushes Katja back into the living room where Gizela is waiting.

"I think you know Gizela, don't you?" Lieutenant Sawyer says. "You like her honey, don't you?" Gizela smiles.

"I am quite sure her husband would like my honey," she says.

Katja is boiling internally.

"Do you know Sasha and Pasha?" Lieutenant Sawyer asks. "What, don't you want to answer anything?"

He moves close to Katja, puts his face next to her ear. "Maybe we are too formal here," he says. "Call me John. Like you wanted to call Hermann's name. Isn't that what lovers do? Go by first names?" Lieutenant Sawyer touches her face and then turns to Sasha and Pasha.

"Go get the kids," he instructs. "Get them all down here. You know, a little accountability. That's how Staff Sergeant Taylor would do it, right?"

Lieutenant Sawyer pulls out a small pistol and points it at Katja.

"Just so you know that I am not playing around tonight," he says. "I got my eye on you, Katja. You like that don't you. A man's eyes watching every curve of your body."

Katja sees the gun and starts to focus all her senses on Lieutenant Sawyer and Gizela. Her adrenaline is pumping so much that she can feel the hair on her arms stand. Every pore in her body is sensing everything. She can almost smell a difference in the air. Her blood is pumping more oxygen to her brain, increasing her awareness of everything. Katja is watching every move they make and thinking of ways to change this outcome.

Rick makes it back to the base and switches vehicles. The Hummer would never drive as fast as his civilian car. He speeds out the gate towards his house. Franz is getting closer and tries to call Rick to deliver Sabine's message to him.

Sabine calls Rick and tells him the situation as the door to Rick and Katja's bedroom opens up. Sabine stands in front of the kids against the far wall. She is still worried about Michael and Katja, but she does not give a show of force or show her weapons. Sasha and Pasha enter the room and Sabine immediately recognizes Pasha. He is the man that killed her husband. Sabine's anger starts brewing and she turns red, her heart racing. Pasha looks at her and smiles.

"I recognize you," he says. "Oh, you are a little widow, aren't you? Sad your husband had to die. It was him or me. You understand, don't you?"

Rage fills Sabine. The kids are all huddled behind her, and Pasha is still about ten feet away from her. Sabine pulls out the pistol with the suppressor from under her arm and sinks a bullet in his forehead.

Sasha starts to move, but Sabine says, "don't move. Don't say a word." The suppressor muffled the sound and smoke starts to leave the tip. The shell casing is still bouncing on the floor.

The kids gasp, Sabine looks at them and holds her finger over her mouth to hush them. Sabine tells Noah to call Michael with the plan and to tell him to start when he hears them talking on the second floor. Noah nods. Sabine looks at Sasha.

"Don't even breathe wrong," she warns. "You will walk down the stairs when we are ready, leading the way. I will be right behind you. If anything goes wrong, I will split your head in two. Do you understand?"

Sasha, silent with fear, nods yes.

Rick has just crossed the bridge closest to the house. He is within three minutes of home with Franz closing in as well.

Katja, Lieutenant Sawyer, and Gizlea are in the living room with Katja's back towards the staircase, and Gizela and Lieutenant Sawyer facing the stairs. Lieutenant Sawyer smiles.

"So, you been looking for me this whole time, and I have been right under your nose," he taunts. "You and Rick suck for spies. I'm a simple chemical guy, and you couldn't figure out that I am the mixer. What a shame."

Lieutenant Sawyer rolls up his sleeve and shakes his head. "No one even asked me about this great tattoo that I swore allegiance to. What a shame. I am a professional and I am stuck screwing around with amateurs. This is embarrassing," he laughs.

Sabine looks at Noah and says, "tell Michael we are moving."

Noah calls Michael. "We are moving when you hear us talking; come upstairs quickly."

"I am ready," Michael tells Noah.

Sabine opens the bedroom door, pushes Sasha out, and whispers, "one slow step at a time. If I want you to move faster, I will tap you," she says. "When you get to the bottom and if there are any questions, you will respond that you have four of the kids and Sabine, understand?"

Sasha nods yes. Sasha starts out of the door with Sabine behind her and Jonas, Emma, Noah, and Sabastian following. They make it down to the second floor, then Sabine nods and the kids start talking.

"Why do we have to go downstairs?" Emma says.

"I want to go back to bed," Noah says.

"What are we doing?" Jonas says.

Katja hears the kids and realizes that something is going on. She is not sure what it is, but she knows that Sabine has control of the situation with the kids. She focuses completely on Lieutenant Sawyer, tuning almost everything else out. Her senses are peaking, and she almost smells the molecules in the air.

Lieutenant Sawyer has a puzzled look on his face, he looks at Katja.

"Your kids are whiny little things, aren't they?" he sneers.

Katja knows something is about to happen. Everything is moving almost in slow motion. She keeps her eyes on Lieutenant Sawyer and Gizlea.

Sasha, Sabine, and the kids slowly start moving down from the second floor. Michael hears the noise and creeps up from the basement with a bat in his hands.

Sasha gets to the bottom of the stairs and Noah yells, "NOW!"

Sabine kicks Sasha to the floor, then shoots Lieutenant Sawyer in the chest. Lieutenant Sawyer falls to the ground and squeezes off a shot that hits Katja in the leg. Jonas steps around Sabine with the second Beretta and shoots Sasha while she is on the ground. Sabine tries for a shot on Gizlea, but Katja's in the way. Michael runs on to the scene and hits Sasha in the back with the bat.

Jonas sees that Katja is hit and screams, "MOM!"

Katja, filled with rage as blood flows from her leg, tackles Gizlea. Sabine sees Lieutenant Sawyer moving slowly, so she shoots him again, this time in the head. The kids notice Katja is bleeding and all start screaming. Sabine pushes all the kids to the kitchen while reassuring them and securely covers the area.

"Shoot anyone coming through the kitchen door and I mean anything," she tells Jonas. "Michael and Jonas protect the rest. I will help your mom."

Sabine walks over to Sasha and pumps a round in the back of her head. She kicks Sasha to roll her over. It is apparent that she is dead. Then Sabine walks over to Lieutenant Sawyer and kicks him over, too. It was obvious he is dead as well. In the living room, Katja is on top of Gizlea and has her by the head, slamming it to the floor over and over. Rage is flowing through Katja's veins at an accelerated pace. Gizlea tries to wiggle out of Katja's hands by grabbing Katja's leg where she was shot. Katja screams in pain, and with every little bit of stamina left she pulls out her dagger, in one fast motion she slices Gizlea's throat. Blood shoots across Katja's face, torso, and the entire room.

Katja looks at Gizlea as the life leaves her body and says, "your fucking lip balm sucks."

The front door opens, and Rick runs in. He looks around to see three bodies lying in front of the stairs. Sabine looks up at Rick.

"Katja has been shot but I think she is okay," she tells him. "I am going upstairs to ensure Pasha is dead. I shot him in the head, but he is the only one we didn't double-check."

Sabine pauses for a second then runs upstairs. Rick hears three suppressed gunshots and, with each shot, Sabine screaming with anger and rage.

Rick runs over to Katja. She is soaked in Gizlea's blood and her own.

"Oh, my love, where have you been shot?" he frantically asks.

Katja lets out a deep breath and touches Rick's face. "It's my leg," she says. "Don't worry, I will be okay."

Rick sees the blood flowing from her left leg. He takes his shirt off, puts it over her wound and applies pressure to help stop the bleeding. Katja is trembling with rage, fear, and excitement.

Sabine walks downstairs and starts crying uncontrollably as she hangs on to the railing for support. "He killed my Hans, my Hans, he killed my Hans," she sobs.

Rick gasps as he hears this and Katja's eyes widen in surprise. Sabine looks at Katja and says, "Oh, my. Are you okay?"

"I will be fine," Katja replies, trying to hide the pain.

"Where are the kids?" Rick asks suddenly. "The kids, where are the kids?"

Sabine still crying, says, "they are in the kitchen."

Rick gets up and makes his way to the kitchen.

"Stop!" Sabine yells. "Don't go in there, they will shoot you." Sabine steps over the bodies at the foot of the staircase and goes to the kitchen door.

"Jonas, it is me, Sabine," she says through the door. "It is safe to come out now. You can open the door, now."

Noah opens the door while Jonas keeps the gun aimed straight ahead, ready to shoot. Michael stands directly behind Jonas with the bat ready to hit someone if Jonas misses the shot. Emma and Sebastian are behind them. Jonas sees Sabine and Rick, then lowers the gun, and the kids come running out.

Franz runs into the house, with his pistol in his hand.

"Is anyone of you hurt?" he asks.

"Katja has been shot in the leg," Rick replies.

Franz takes a quick look at her leg, and says, "She will be fine, I will have a medical team here in a few."

Rick looks around to make sure everyone in the family is there.

"Rick and Katja," Sabine says, still crying. "I am sorry if you are mad at me for involving the children. I couldn't figure another way to get out of this. This was the only way I could think of."

Katja grabs Sabine, hugs her, and then kisses her graciously on her cheeks. Rick looks at everyone, then slowly looks across the room to where the bodies are. Taking in what just happened, he looks at everyone and says, "Nothing comes between our family!"

FINALÉ

SEVENTEEN YEARS LATER IN 2021.

Rick and Katja slowly walk off the Old Bridge. The beautiful scenery around the river and bridge quickly intoxicates the people that are there.

"Rick let's walk back to our old house along the river, just one more time," Katja says. As they walk along the river, Rick stops Katja.

"Katja, do you understand when a man looks into your eyes what those do to a man?" he asks.

Katja smiles and looks deeply into his blues eyes, she caresses his face and leans to his ear, and with a whisper, she says, "tell me, Rick, what do my eyes do?" Rick smiles and leans back to kiss her.

After they kiss, Katja chuckles, and Rick looks at her, confused.

"You realize you just kissed me where we pushed Kristoff into the river," Katja says. Rick laughs and gives a satisfying smile.

"Our life just blossomed right here, my love," Katja says. "I want you to know this, and I have said it before, but it is only fitting Rick. Even though I have fantasies about wild guys and unknown men, you are the only man I want in me."

Rick touches his heart. "Oh, my love, you say the sweetest things."

Rick turns to look back at the Café by the Corner of the Bridge, one more time. The scent of tobacco slowly fills the air. Rick recognizes the aroma as it takes over his senses. He starts to smile. Rick realizes exactly where that smell comes from.

Faintly, a recognizable voice says, "Hallo, my friends, it's been some time."

Katja turns to see a familiar silhouette and smiles.

THE END.